DREAM HOUSE

DREAM HOUSE

A Novel by CutiePieMarzia

MARZIA BISOGNIN

Keywords
PRESS

—

ATRIA

NEW YORK   LONDON   TORONTO   SYDNEY   NEW DELHI

An Imprint of Simon & Schuster, Inc.
1230 Avenue of the Americas
New York, NY 10020

First Keywords Press hardcover edition April 2016

Keywords Press/Atria Books and colophons are trademarks of Simon & Schuster, Inc.

For information about special discounts for bulk purchases, please contact Simon & Schuster Special Sales at 1-866-506-1949 or business@simonandschuster.com.

The Simon & Schuster Speakers Bureau can bring authors to your live event. For more information or to book an event, contact the Simon & Schuster Speakers Bureau at 1-866-248-3049 or visit our website at www.simonspeakers.com.

Manufactured in the United States of America

10 9 8 7 6 5 4 3 2 1

Library of Congress Cataloging-in-Publication Data

Names: Bisognin, Marzia.
Title: Dream house : a CutiePieMarzia novel / Marzia Bisognin.
Description: First Keywords Press hardcover edition. | New York : Atria/Keywords Press, [2016] | Summary: A young woman's dream house quickly becomes a nightmare.
Identifiers: LCCN 2015047499 (print) | LCCN 2016004034 (ebook) | ISBN 9781501135262 (hardback) | ISBN 9781501135286 (E-Book)
Subjects: | CYAC: Supernatural—Fiction. | Haunted houses—Fiction. | BISAC: JUVENILE FICTION / General.
Classification: LCC PZ7.1.B556 Dr 2016 (print) | LCC PZ7.1.B556 (ebook) | DDC [Fic]—dc23
LC record available at http://lccn.loc.gov/2015047499

ISBN 978-1-5011-3526-2
ISBN 978-1-5011-3528-6 (ebook)

To my family, who have always allowed me to
express my creativity freely.
To Felix, my partner, who believes in me
and keeps me positive.
To my marzipans, who never fail to support me.

DREAM HOUSE

DAY 1

THERE IT is, right in front of me.

A one-story Greek Revival house, probably dating back to the early 1900s by the look of it.

From the gate, a path of small flagstones crosses the front garden, ending at three small steps which lead up to the porch. A row of columns supporting a triangular pediment with a small bull's-eye window adorn the façade, and between them I can see a rocking chair among the potted plants.

The whole thing is painted a luminous white, which is set off by the pale blue of the shutters flanking its narrow windows. It's surrounded by neatly trimmed green lawns, perfectly tonsured hedges, and immaculate flowerbeds, and they all suit the place perfectly.

A thin trail of smoke rises from the chimney on the pointed roof. To one side, the top of a white church spire peeks out from behind distant trees, while to the other, the dark tiles of a neighbour's roof are visible.

I somehow have the strangest sensation that this is all I have ever dreamt of, ever since I was just a little girl—of owning a modest yet exquisite house, a house like this, surrounded by fields and the odd neighbour. And now it seems as though the image that I've been gradually assembling in my mind since childhood has come vividly to life right in front of me, just so that I can admire it in all of its splendour.

I stand there by the black iron gate that separates me from the tidy garden and stare at the doorbell, an elegant little gold button set below a brass nameplate that, evidently, no one has ever bothered to use, undisturbed as it is by a name.

The unengraved nameplate might suggest there's nobody currently living in the house, but the sight of the well-kept grounds gives the lie to the idea—and holds me there, transfixed.

Perfectly still.

Immobile.

Frozen.

Wondering how exactly I even arrived here in the first place.

I've never noticed this house before, and yet it's always been right where it is. I know that.

Somehow.

Blanketed by the woolly clouds of deepening autumn, the sky is getting darker and darker by the second. That's the way it feels, at least, although I don't really have any idea how long I've actually been standing here, my finger suspended in mid-air, aimed at that lonely button.

The air is heavy with a powerful smell, something that I recognise, something that makes me think of . . . lawnmowers? Is it oil? Or maybe kerosene?

I don't even know what it is I'm standing here waiting for, but there's definitely something holding me back from ringing the bell; it's as if I'm not *supposed* to be here now, in this particular moment.

Here I am, though, stuck under this darkening sky, and so I eventually decide to force myself to go through with it. I close my eyes, take a deep breath, and begin to move my finger forward.

But before it gets close enough to make contact, I hear a worried voice from nearby asking, "Are you all right?"

My eyes snap open and I see an elderly couple standing on the front porch, which just a minute before I'd been admiring with such intensity. I stare at them, not uttering a single word.

Looking increasingly unnerved, the lady slowly descends the steps and walks down the path towards me, the old man close behind her. She's not looking at *me*, though—her eyes seem to be focused on something over my shoulder.

Mine remain locked upon her.

She reaches the gate and—looking me full in the face now, her eyes quite concerned—repeats, "Are you all right, dear? You really shouldn't be standing out here in the rain."

I gaze down at the grey paving stones beneath my feet and notice that, yes, they're rapidly becoming freckled with dark, wet spots. Before I can say anything, the tall gentleman accompanying her opens the gate and puts his arm around me, implying an invitation to enter what I suppose is their lovely home.

Once we're safely inside, the front door closes behind us and I'm ushered over to the sofa near the fireplace. I can't stop looking around the room in which I now find myself—a medium-sized parlour with a high, embossed ceiling, its Victorian décor illuminated by two large French windows and a crystal chandelier.

It truly is my dream house. It just happens to already belong to someone else.

While I make myself cosy, the kindly old lady disappears for a minute, and with shaky hands the old man puts some logs on the fire in an attempt to bring the dying embers back to life.

Strangely enough, I have the feeling now that I am exactly where I'm supposed to be—not like before. And I don't want to leave. Even though I know that very soon I'll have to, and that I don't actually have any real excuse for being here to begin with.

As I sit on the stiff leather sofa, still peering in wonder around the beautiful room, I realise that the couple who live here must be religious, because the walls and bookshelves are dotted with symbols whose meanings I'm not exactly sure of but which I'm absolutely certain are esoteric.

I ask myself why on earth they would be so nice to me, why they would so happily invite a complete stranger inside their home, but then I think, *What am I complaining about? I wanted to go inside, didn't I?*

The sweet-looking lady appears again. She places a cup of hot tea on the coffee table in front of me and clears her throat as she takes a seat at the opposite end of the sofa. She's fair-skinned with hazel eyes, and her hair—short and fluffy, its original auburn colour now fading—suits the healthy pink glow of her cheeks. The smile on her face seems forced, though, betraying a tension she's trying carefully to hide.

I reach for the cup and feel its warmth between my fingers.

"I'm Amabel," she says. "And this"—pointing at the man who is now standing by the door with an open book in his hands—"is my husband, Marvin. Nice to have you in our home."

Giving me a distracted smile, Marvin nods.

I open my mouth, but no words come out, so instead I bring the cup to my lips and take a slow sip, bothered and confused at the same time.

What is wrong *with me?*

I've always been aware of the fact that I'm not exactly what you might call a particularly . . . *sociable* person. But I'm definitely not *rude*. And yet that's exactly the way I'm behaving towards these people.

Why?

But before I get a chance to ponder the question further, Amabel stands up and walks across to the other side of the room to join her husband.

"It's getting late," she says, "and there's a storm forecast for tonight. You are very welcome to spend the night here. I'll take you to the guest room. I hope you'll find it comfortable in there."

Finding myself unable to reply, I decide that the least I can do is go along with the invitation, and so I nod meekly and get up to follow her. As we walk past Marvin, who is still intent on his reading, I manage a quick peek at the embossed title of the volume he is holding—*Spiritual Relief.*

The carpeted floor creaks beneath our feet as we make our way along the corridor which leads away from the living room. The walls are wainscotted and hung with artworks and the odd photo, and at the end of the corridor is the door to a little spare room, isolated from the rest of the house. Now looking visibly pleased to have me there, Amabel holds it open for me.

As I step past her and go inside I manage a gesture with my head that's meant to show my gratitude, and while she closes the door she gives me a smile in return that seems both happy and melancholy.

I potter around that solitary yet cosy little room for a while, trying not to dwell too much upon what a strange situation I find myself in, but at the same time quite unable to fathom what has happened.

In the end, I lay myself down on what turns out to be a surprisingly comfortable bed and do my best to relax.

The sound of the breeze blowing softly through the slightly open window by the bed makes me sleepy, and so I decide to switch off the Tiffany lamp that, together with a small alarm clock, occupies the nightstand.

A few moments later I feel my tired, heavy eyes closing, allowing me to get some rest for the night.

DAY 2

AFRIGHTENINGLY LOUD crash-ing noise awakens me from what seemed to be a weird yet wonderful dream, and I'm surprised to find that I am actually still here, in the same room where I went to sleep. It is real, after all.

Hugging the pillow, I turn my head to the bedside table in search of the clock.

It says 3:00 p.m.

How can I possibly have slept for so long? Is the clock wrong, or can that really be the right time?

I jump out of bed and rush over to open the door, revealing the quiet corridor I walked down last night. I make my way to the living room, but there's no one there, and the only sounds filling the emptiness around me are the rain rattling incessantly at the windows and the soft ticking of the grandfather clock that stands near the door.

In that soft grey light, the house looks completely different; even though everything is still exactly as it was, it no longer feels like the lovely, warm home I'd snatched a glimpse of the previous day. It's not quite as *homely*, almost as if it were . . . abandoned.

No, that can't be right.

The couple I had the pleasure of meeting must have worked hard to create this love nest of theirs, and there's no conceivable reason for them to have just walked out on it, especially not after being so hospitable to me, especially not today.

They wouldn't just *leave* me.

Would they?

They probably went out; that would explain it. It is Monday, after all, and people have things to do. Not *me*, but normal people. Jobs, chores, shopping, walking the dog.

Personally, I don't even know where I'm *supposed* to be.

Would anyone care where I am?

What do I usually do with my time?

Dozens of questions suddenly start popping into my brain, and at the violent blizzard of thoughts my head starts pounding, as though it's in some way wrong of me to want to know the answers.

Standing in the centre of the very same room where yesterday I'd sat drinking my hot tea, I suddenly begin to feel dizzy—both cold and sweaty at the same time—and a second later I find myself lying facedown on the floor, my palms flat against the chilly wooden floorboards.

My eyelids start to grow impossibly heavy, and despite struggling with all my strength to keep them open I only manage to give myself a few extra seconds of blurry vision before they're forced shut.

And in those few seconds, I see something.

A pair of feet, clad in shiny Oxford shoes.

Right before I lose consciousness.

◎◎

A loud knocking on the door brings me back round.

When I open my eyes, everything is dark.

I lie there for a few seconds, trying to come up with a plausible explanation for what just happened.

Maybe I'm sick?

I certainly don't feel too great. I haven't had anything to eat for ages—perhaps I just passed out because of that. I probably ought to have something . . . but why is everything so dark? Am I still alone?

I stop, draw in a deep breath, and then slowly let it back out.

From outside there's the sound of rain pattering on the roof and splashing from the gutters.

Sluggishly, I climb to my feet. And realize, when I hear a renewed burst of loud knocks, that whoever is outside of the house is still trying to get my attention. Summoning all of my strength, I drag myself over to the front door and, to my surprise, manage to open it without difficulty, only to find a petite woman standing on the porch who, by the looks of her, is well into her eighties. In her hand she holds a huge black umbrella, which she has been using to shelter her small body from the rain.

Our eyes meet, she, seemingly, as surprised to see me opening the door as I am to find her on the other side of it, and for a moment this bizarre tableau remains motionless.

The old lady makes the first move: without uttering a word, she points her index finger right at me, between my eyes, and then turns around.

Puzzled, I watch her back as she slowly trots away down the steps and along the path towards the gate, the raindrops splashing off her umbrella, and then I set off after her.

When I'm halfway across the garden I turn to look behind me, wondering if I really should leave the house.

But why should I stay?

Unable to come up with any convincing reason, I turn back around and continue down the path again, ready to go.

It takes me a moment to realise that the old woman isn't there anymore—all about me there's only darkness, and the only thing I can see ahead is the gate, which has been left open.

I walk over to have a better look at it, but as soon as I touch its iron frame a weird sensation—something almost like a shiver of disgust, or of horror—runs through my entire body, and I back away quickly, feeling strangely upset and vaguely nauseous.

I shouldn't leave, I tell myself, hurriedly pushing the gate closed with my foot and rushing back to the house through the rain. I slam the door shut and flick the switch to the enormous chandelier floating up there near the ceiling, and the room instantly springs to life, giving me a feeling of warmth and welcome almost as strongly as it did the previous day.

Even though I'm starving, there's something more pressing that needs dealing with right away: getting hold of some dry clothes; after being out in the rain, the ones I am wearing—literally my only belongings—are now soaked through.

Dripping all over the floor, I walk through the corridors of the house turning on the lights and eventually find myself back in what is, for the moment at least, my bedroom.

I open the wardrobe: there's a pair of soft pyjamas covered in pictures of bunny rabbits hiding in their burrows. They're not ideal but they're good enough, and when I put them on I find that they fit me perfectly.

There's an ideal spot for drying my wet clothes on the radiator underneath the window, so I borrow a few hangers from the wardrobe and use them to hang my green army jacket and plain white T-shirt as well as I can against the hot metal, dumping my black jeans untidily on top.

Gradually starting to warm up again, I find myself back in the kitchen, which opens onto the living room, and hunt through the cupboards, drawers, and shiny chrome fridge for a snack. Just like with the pyjamas, there isn't much choice—but probably still more than I've really got any right to expect. I opt for the packet of tortilla chips I find, pour some into a bowl, and walk into the parlour.

As I snuggle down to tuck in to my food, I realise that I'm starting to grow fond of this stiff old sofa, and it begins to dawn on me that the thing I'd been secretly hoping for is actually becoming reality: the house of my dreams is all for me.

If it weren't for the strangeness of the whole situation, I would still think that I was dreaming.

❦

After finishing off the tortilla chips, I place the bowl on the coffee table by the sofa and walk over to the French windows.

The rain is still pouring down and night has swallowed up the outside world, but I spot a light on the other side of the hedge which runs around the border of the back garden.

The neighbours.

Perhaps they have the answers to some of my questions. There's a small chance that they might know where the owners have gone, at least.

I look for an umbrella, find one in the wooden cupboard in the entrance hall, slip on my sneakers, and make my way outside. I'm standing at the front of the house now, the side that I'm acquainted with, but I'll need to walk round to the back if I want to get a better view of the neighbours' property and find out how to reach them.

I start making my way across the wet grass, staying close to the thick walls of the house, and make my first left turn, eyeing as I pass it the small window of the room I slept in. Another left turn is all it takes to reach my destination, and so—treading carefully through the darkness—there I am.

There's nothing to light my way out here, but I follow the path and soon enough find myself standing in the middle of the damp back garden, looking at the yellow light that cuts through the blackness.

There's no movement visible through the neighbours' windows, but to the right, a small wooden gate in the hedge seems to connect the two properties. At the other end of the garden, half-hidden by some bushes, I spot a small shed, very similar in appearance to the house itself but much smaller.

I spend a moment deciding what would be the best course of action: should I enter the neighbours' property, or go and take a look at that tiny shed? Neither option is particularly enticing, but at a loss as to what else to do, I start walking over towards the corner of the garden where the little wooden hut sits.

Before I get very far, though, I hear a sound from behind me.

I spin around and freeze in my tracks at the sight of a shadowy form in one of the two big living room windows of Amabel and Marvin's house.

Just like me, the indistinct figure freezes for an instant. The only thing I can see clearly is a hand touching the glass; everything else is too dark and blurry to make out. All I know is that someone—or something—is inside that room, inside the house, and that I can't just stand here—I need to do something, fast.

But by the time I've run over to the window, the shadow has gone. It doesn't mean that whoever is inside has left, though.

Frightened, I dump the umbrella on the ground and run back round to the front door, pushing it open to find myself standing in the self-same room as the shadow which had seemed to be watching me. I switch the lights on, and the chandelier immediately illuminates the parlour, but nothing seems to be out of the ordinary in any way: everything is just as I left it.

I know I saw something.

Or at least, I *think* I did.

But could it just be all the pressure that I'm under? Could it simply be that I *imagined* it?

Gingerly, I cross the room, raise my left hand, and rest it against the windowpane, feeling the cold glass under my palm. My head is still aching from before, reeling from this flood of strange new events.

With my hand still pressed against the window and my

eyes closed, I try to decide what I should do next. Leave? Just because the people living here were so nice to me, that doesn't really give me any right to be in their house. But at the same time, I want to at least thank them for their hospitality last night. Maybe they've left a note for me somewhere, and all I need to do is find it. Despite feeling like I'd rather just curl up on the sofa, I force myself to wander through those empty corridors once again in search of any messages that might have been left in the other rooms of the house.

As soon as I take my first step, however, something catches my eye.

The bowl.

The one I'd left on the coffee table. It's no longer there.

It's stacked tidily on a kitchen shelf.

Uncertainly, I give it a good looking over to make sure it's the same one I ate my snack from, and even though it's a perfectly run-of-the-mill glass bowl with no exceptional distinguishing features that might give me the confirmation I seek, the one that was on the table still isn't there.

It's enough to make me feel certain that I'm not imagining it: someone else is in here.

And that person must still be hiding within these walls.

DAY 3

THE OLD grandfather clock's chimes begin to play their melody, telling me that it's midnight, and well past time to begin my search.

I run to the kitchen counter and grab a carving knife from the knife block before cautiously setting off to explore the part of the house that I've not yet set foot in.

Turning left from the front door, a corridor similar to the one that leads to the little room on the right of the house where I slept trails off towards further unknown places. Before me are shut doors, set close to one another.

At first they all look the same, but then I notice that the

door to my left doesn't bear a sign identifying its function, unlike the two to my right.

Knife gripped tightly in my left hand, I take hold of the doorknob with my right and give it a quick twist. It's locked.

I try again, this time applying more pressure, but it doesn't make any difference—it's not opening.

Is that . . . ?

I put my ear to the wooden panelling.

A voice.

A whispering voice.

I leap back, startled.

I'm absolutely certain that whoever was in the living room is now on the other side of this door. I kneel down, bending as low as I possibly can until my right eye is squinting through the crack underneath.

There they are—the same feet I saw before I fainted!

At this point, whoever is hiding in there might well be the only person able to tell me what is going on. And I need to know.

Totally at a loss as to what else to do, I climb to my feet and start banging desperately on the door as hard as I can, as though the only thing I care about in the world—the only thing that matters—is getting to the other side.

Until, suddenly, I hear the key turning in the lock.

I twist the handle and slowly push the door open, trying as I do to gather my thoughts into some kind of an intelligible question for the person I'm expecting to find standing there waiting for me.

But when I'm finally ready, the only thing I see before me is a staircase: about ten steps leading down into the darkness beneath the ground floor.

It takes my eyes a few seconds to adjust to the gloom, but I summon up all of my courage and start to descend, the knife held out in front of me in my trembling hand. The old wooden slats creak loudly beneath my feet at each step, almost drowning out the sound of the rain outside.

As I go, I gradually become aware of a vague glow coming from below.

When I've almost reached the bottom of the steps, I see the small cellar I am about to enter to my right. The room is illuminated by candles burning in each corner, as well as by others propped on shelves and brackets all over the walls. I pick one up to light my way and advance towards the centre of the room, where a white circle has been drawn in chalk onto the rough flagstones of the floor.

The cellar is obviously used as a storeroom—the walls are lined with old chairs with threadbare upholstery, decrepit cupboards, and overflowing cardboard boxes.

I'm standing by the chalk line and peering about me in search of the mysterious person when I feel two hands take me by the shoulders and forcefully shove me forward, into the circle.

Things start to happen in quick succession—first, I hear footsteps running up the stairs. Then, somehow, something suddenly blows out all of the candles at once, leaving me in pitch darkness.

And then I hear the basement door slam shut.

Dimly aware of a kind of murmuring noise behind me, I blindly bump my way through the junk and old furniture littering the floor and hurry as quickly as I can to the foot of the stairs. When I finally reach them, I start racing up towards the cellar door.

It's then that something grabs hold of one of my ankles.

Its grip is icy cold, and whatever it is drags me violently back down the stairs, back to the centre of the storeroom.

What had begun as whispers grow louder and more intense until they've turned into full-blown screams, and in this maelstrom of noise, my body spins around the room in complete pitch darkness, an awful nightmare coming to actual, horrible life, until finally I give in and stop fighting.

☙

When I come round, I'm sore all over and there's a weird taste in my mouth.

Sunbeams shining through the small window set high in the basement wall are playing on my face and warming my cheeks.

I sit up and look myself over: my ankle is covered in bright red welts and I feel completely drained of strength. Taking a deep breath, I manage to hoist myself to my feet and slowly climb back up the stairs.

I turn the handle of the cellar door and walk along the corridor until I reach the main part of the house, hoping that, as a new day has begun, I'll find either Amabel or Marvin there. In the kitchen, I look at the old ticking clock, which now says 1:54 p.m.

Even though my stomach isn't totally in agreement, I know that I need to get my strength back, and so I force myself to find something to eat, opting for some fruit.

Passing the fridge, I see that one of the black magnetic letters attached to it—this one in the shape of an A—is holding up a note. It says, *See you at dinner. Love, Amabel.*

So they *are* coming back!

She probably came home this morning and left this note for her husband. Maybe she thought I'd already gone?

Feeling relatively reassured, I try to put whatever it was that happened down there in the cellar out of my mind and walk along the hall to my bedroom, where I change back into my now dry clothes, put the pyjamas back in the wardrobe where I found them, and lie down on the bed, flooded with conflicting emotions. The events of the last few days have been strange and, at times, terrifying, but a part of me can't help but be pulled in by this place. I can barely make sense of my own feelings, but I decide that it's worth waiting for Amabel and Marvin to return to get some answers.

I gaze upwards, enchanted by the moulded flower motif which runs along the coving. From the centre of the ceiling hangs a small bronze chandelier which adds a sophisticated touch to the bedroom's already polished design.

To my right, there's the tiny window that overlooks the side garden, and at the foot of the bed the empty wooden wardrobe faces me, drawing my attention to the left side of the room, where, beside the door, is a Provençal desk bearing a mirror.

A shabby-chic interior like this would normally be a bit over the top for a guest room, but the taste shown in the rest of the house explains their decision to use such splendid pieces in this out-of-the-way corner of their home. The whole place is extremely well kept—exactly the way I imagined it would be when, standing outside two days ago, I first saw it. Before I knew what was to come.

Bored of lying down, I get up and walk over to the desk to examine myself in the mirror: the light green of my eyes is accentuated by the dark rings forming beneath them; my wavy brown hair, hanging loose over my shoulders, looks dull; and my skin seems even paler than usual.

As I'm staring at my sallow features, I hear a noise coming from the hall. I look at the clock and see that the time is 7:37, so I set off towards the parlour to welcome Amabel back.

I sit down in the comfortable armchair next to the couch and wait impatiently for her to come in, growing gradually more and more concerned by how long she's taking.

She must be doing something on the porch. Perhaps she's chatting with a neighbour?

A few minutes later, I hear the noise again. I look over at the doorknob and see from its rattling that she's trying to open the door but without success, so I get up from my chair and walk over to open it for her—and am unpleasantly surprised to find that the person outside is not the one I was expecting.

It's the same elderly lady from last night, this time without her black umbrella but with a pair of thick tortoiseshell glasses framing her petite face. Staring up at me, she once again raises her finger, then—without taking her eyes off mine—pulls her arm back until it is pointing towards the half-open gate.

The wrinkles on her forehead deepen, forming an expression of acute distress.

"How can I help you?" I finally manage to say. "Would you like to come inside?" I gesture with my head to the warm parlour.

But by the time I turn back to her she's gone again, and the gate is closed.

I shut the door, wondering why on earth this strange woman keeps appearing. But not for long, as soon my thoughts turn to worrying about getting something to eat and finding a bathtub to wash myself in.

I remember reading "Bathroom" on a door right opposite the door to the cellar earlier on, so after snacking on a packet of crackers I find in one of the kitchen cupboards, I grab my pyjamas and set off in that direction.

There I am again, back before those three doors—but this time I open the one to the right and start preparing for a well-deserved bath.

I dump my clothes on the floor, turn the hot water tap full on, and, once the tub is full, lower myself into it, feeling myself relax for the first time since my arrival. The sensation is so sweet that I go one step farther: holding my breath, I let my head slide beneath the surface. With the water caressing me more closely than anything has in a long time, insulating me from the confusing outside world, I can hear every single movement my body makes.

I can't remember the last time I felt like this. So calm, without a single thought in my head.

It truly is the sweetest moment I have experienced in the last few days—until it's ruined by the bathroom light suddenly going out with a little fizzing noise, leaving me in what would be complete darkness were it not for the window high over the tub.

I don't want to let this get to me—I need this tranquillity to last a bit longer. And so, repeating to myself "It's totally normal; there's nothing to worry about," I leap out of the water and flick the switch a couple of times until the lights come back on and I can climb back into the lovely hot water to enjoy another fifteen minutes of peace.

Finally, when I'm on the verge of dozing off, I reach over

the side of the tub and grab from the rack a large bath towel, which I quickly wrap around myself. And as I do so it occurs to me that I can't stay here. The food is going to run out soon if nobody comes back, and there's no sign of those regular everyday things you need, like a toothbrush. . . .

Except that there is.

A third, brand-new toothbrush, still in its unopened packet, is sitting right there in the glass near the sink, next to two others that have evidently already seen a bit of action.

That's lucky.

I pull it out and put it to use, relishing the minty flavour of the toothpaste in my mouth before spitting out the frothy water and taking one last good look at myself in the mirror, where I see that I'm still looking exhausted.

Then I leave the bathroom and climb into my soft bed.

DAY 4

IN THE middle of the night, I'm awoken by a noise coming from somewhere inside the room.

Inside my bedroom.

I screw my eyes tightly shut and hope that it will go away.

It doesn't, of course. It's still there—a sound like something scratching, scratching incessantly.

I force my eyelids open and peek out over the covers to try to get an idea of where it's coming from, only to realize that its source is much closer than I'd thought: it's coming from inside the wardrobe.

I clutch the top of the blanket tightly, and the scratching sound abruptly vanishes, leaving me staring at the wardrobe's closed doors until, a few seconds later, somebody starts crying—so softly it almost sounds like hiccupping.

So softly it sends chills down my spine.

I lie there in the bed, petrified and completely motionless, with only my eyes peeping out over the covers, while whoever is in the wardrobe sobs away.

Somehow, I gradually manage to calm myself down and force myself to accept that, even though the situation makes absolutely no sense—no sense at all—there isn't any real reason for me to be afraid. Throwing the blankets aside, I set one foot warily after the other and slowly cross the carpet, moving closer and closer to the large wooden wardrobe until eventually I'm grasping its door handles.

I don't know what it is I'm expecting. To be honest, I don't even really *have* any expectations, because I don't want to let the thought that something awful might be hiding in there unnerve me.

And so in one smooth, decisive motion, I throw both wardrobe doors wide open—and gaze uncomprehendingly at the little girl I find crouching within, huddled up and weeping in a corner under the jangling coat hangers.

Her face is streaked with tears, and she is tightly hugging a soft toy—a white bunny rabbit with a bit of thread where one of its eyes used to be. She looks up at me.

"Where are they?" she asks pleadingly. "Why would they leave me?"

Not knowing what to answer, nor even to whom she's referring, I offer her my hand. She reaches out and takes it, letting me lead her from the wardrobe over to the bed. I sit her down on top of the covers and, perching myself next to her, ask her what she was doing in there.

With lowered eyes she turns her head away, saying only, "They left me."

Seeing that she's struggling to choke back her tears, I wait for a few seconds before asking my next question.

"How long have you been in there?"

This time she looks me directly in the face and answers candidly, "I don't know."

I tell her to stay there on the bed while I make us both some hot tea, and then head for the kitchen with the hope of giving myself a couple of minutes to think the situation through and maybe get some idea of what on earth is going on.

Plenty of ideas do in fact come to mind while the kettle boils on the hob—but unfortunately none of them actually makes any sense, so I just focus on preparing the drinks and getting back to check on her as quickly as I'm able.

I place the cups on a tray, along with a little sugar bowl and a couple of teaspoons, and set off down the darkening corridor. As my bare feet tread the creaking floor, the only thing I can see in front of me is the crack of light coming from around the door I'm slowly approaching.

Unexpectedly, a weird sensation suddenly rushes through my entire body for a second, making me shiver violently.

Something is wrong.

As the thought takes root in my mind, I start walking faster and faster until I reach the bedroom door. With one foot, I push it open, then freeze in my tracks, in total shock at the terrible obscenity of what I am seeing.

Fighting desperately to breathe, the little girl is hanging in mid-air, a thin, taut cord running from around her throat up to the chandelier. Her feet kick desperately against nothing.

Overcome by panic, I drop the tray, and the teacups and sugar and spoons clatter to the floor. "No!" I scream the word as I run across the room and scramble up onto the bed, my fingers fumbling ineffectually at the knotted rope around her tiny neck, doing my best to release her.

"Now it's too late," she whispers, her frenzied thrashing slowing. "They will never know I exist."

And just like that, she exhales her last breath.

Somehow I manage to get her down, and, still crying with shock, sit on the bed with her little body cradled in my arms, squeezing her tightly to my chest as if maybe the beating of my heart might bring her back to life.

But she's not moving anymore.

I scream one more time. "NO!"

. . . and then wake up to see the polished wood of the furniture glowing in the weak sunlight. I am alone. There's no body.

It was a nightmare. An absolutely awful nightmare.

❧

It takes a while for me to accept that the whole thing was all in my head, that it wasn't actually real—but I can't stop thinking about it.

What could it have meant? I didn't know that little girl, yet I felt such a bond with her; I needed to save her. And if I hadn't left the room, she wouldn't have died.

I should have stayed with her.

It was *my* fault!

Over and over again, I replay the scene in my mind,

getting more upset each time but never quite managing to squeeze any kind of meaning out of it.

Finally, I shake my head in defeat.

Realising from the rumblings of my stomach that it's already lunchtime, I walk back through the living room and into the kitchen. The note on the fridge isn't there anymore, adding yet another mystery to the others already crowding my mind, but I ignore the thought and start assembling a plateful of mixed snacks while I enjoy the view over the back garden and the house next door. Now that the sun is shining, I can clearly see the gate which connects the two properties, and it makes me wonder if I will ever get a chance to meet the neighbours.

After everything that's happened, I feel the need to know more about all these strange events. As much as I would like them to stop, I need to understand the situation I'm in—and I don't feel like I can just walk away from it.

There's so much on my mind—and none of it straightforward—that it starts to feel almost as though the air itself is thickening around me, until finally it gets to the point that I absolutely need some fresh air. I dump my plate on the kitchen counter, put on my sneakers, and—still in my pyjamas—prepare to step outside.

I pause by the open door for a moment to stretch and notice a small pile of newspapers and magazines lying there on the floor: the *Evening Hills*, the *White Hills Advertiser*, *The Clerical Gazette*. . . .

I pick them up, heap them all together next to the old black Bakelite telephone on the graceful little hall table by the entrance, then let myself out and take the same path as a few nights previous until I find myself standing by the white wooden gate, where I can see the neighbours' house up close.

It's a massive-looking thing, which appears to have three floors above ground and the added space of a tower protruding from its side. The small, sunken windows contrast with the mansion's imposing appearance, and the green ivy leaves hugging the tower's walls seem almost to be strangling it, except where they thin out lower down towards the ground, allowing the grey colour of the stone to show through.

I turn around to admire once again the gorgeous windows of my dream house and sink down until I am sitting on the ground with my back resting against the gate, letting myself bask in all that loveliness.

Everything is quiet, the only noise that of a faraway train passing by, lending a magical touch to the already perfect scenery—until this idyllic moment is interrupted by a finger tapping me gently on the shoulder. I jump in surprise and turn to see who the finger belongs to.

On the other side of the gate, a young man—probably in his early twenties—is standing there smiling down at me.

"Hey," he says, while I'm still recovering from the fright.

"I didn't think anyone was here," I manage to mumble. "I . . . I—"

He cuts me off reassuringly. "Oh, don't worry—I've only just got here myself."

His grey eyes are mesmerizing, and a perfect match for the stone of the house in the background. His short, dark hair is messy, and even though the broad smile is still there on his face, there's a look in his eyes that expresses a profound sadness.

"Do you live in that house?" I ask out of curiosity.

"Yes. Yes, I'm stuck in there," he confirms. "But it's not that bad."

Worried that I might have sounded rude, I counter, "Oh, I think it's rather interesting."

He looks at the house for a few seconds and then bursts out laughing. Taken aback at first by his reaction, I soon let myself go as well and join in with him.

He looks back at me again, his smile fading.

"Well, it was nice talking to you," he says, "but I'm afraid I have to go now. I'm Avery, by the way."

"I'm Amethyst," I reply. "Nice to meet you."

As he walks away, he gives me one last smile over his shoulder before disappearing around the ivy-covered corner of his home.

In the forbidding sky, the gathering grey clouds obscure the last glow of the sunset and hint to me that the time to get back inside has arrived.

I walk back round to the front, picking up the umbrella I'd dropped in fright the other night.

Since it's getting dark—and given my experiences from nights past—I lock the front door behind me and make sure that none of the windows are left open. I want to avoid stumbling across any more unwanted people around the house, real or imagined.

I turn on the TV and, after flicking through a few channels, settle on a cartoon, which does something to help lighten my mood and make me feel less lonely—so much so, in fact, that after a while I decide to prepare myself a nice dinner. I find some vegetables in the fridge and some strawberries with cream. Feeling a bit guilty about eating my way through someone else's food, I promise myself that I will cook a special meal for Amabel and Marvin once they get back.

For the first time since I arrived in this house, I don't feel anxious. Sitting on the firm sofa, I see a light come on outside: it's the same one as last night, and it's coming from Avery's house. Somehow, knowing that somebody is in there makes me feel reassured.

I clean up the kitchen, make a short stop-off in the bathroom, and then walk on to my bedroom to let my body rest for the night.

DAY 5

I CLIMB OUT of bed at 10:37 the next morning and, without even changing into my clothes, walk down the corridor to the kitchen and prepare myself some oatmeal and a glass of milk for breakfast. I sit down at the kitchen table, and as I eat I gaze out of the window at the pretty lawn, now shiny and lustrous with the previous night's rain and kissed by the pale autumnal sunlight.

It's a strangely warm day considering that it's the first week of October—so nice, in fact, that I pick up my glass of milk and walk out onto the front porch, where the rocking chair sits, seemingly waiting for me.

I make myself comfortable in it, and as I drink my milk my eyes gradually wander from the house and its grounds to what lies outside: from the gate to the horizon, multitudes of vast cornfields dotted with countless half-bare trees of all types stretch off into the distance, the whole forming a colourful patchwork.

As I sit there sipping from my glass, a gang of kids runs into view, cheerfully kicking a ball down the opposite pavement.

One of them stops right across the road from me and, hands on hips, stares thoughtfully at something in the road in front of the house for a second. What can he be looking at? An animal? Maybe a hedgehog or something? But the shouts of his friends soon send him racing off after them, whatever it was already forgotten.

Noticing that another wad of newspapers and magazines has been pushed under the gate, I decide to go and collect them. I climb out of the rocking chair and, without putting on my shoes, make my way barefoot down the cold stone path that crosses the garden and connects the porch to the gateway.

The frosty flagstones freeze my feet more with each step I take, but I don't mind—the chill pushes my sleepiness away and makes me feel more awake.

I bring the papers inside and stack them on top of the pile by the entrance hall, together with the ones I dumped there yesterday, before heading over to the sink to wash the dishes.

A sound coming from behind me shatters the silence.

I spin round. Someone is here—this time I am positive of it.

I walk over to the open French windows and study the man I see outside standing by the old shed.

He looks tired, and is probably in his forties, his red hair partially covered by a flat black cap that matches the loose shirt he's wearing. He's pushing a wheelbarrow full of plants.

Soon enough, he notices me looking at him from the window, and his expression changes immediately from one of intent solemnity to a mixture of astonishment and fear. I wave cheerfully to him, certain now that he must be employed here, just as his attire would suggest. Slipping my shoes on, I walk outside and, an inquiring look on my face, introduce myself.

"Hi. I hope you didn't think I was spying on you. I'm Amethyst; nice to meet you!" I venture.

He gives me a good looking over from head to toe, taking a moment longer than is really polite, before replying peevishly, "How are Mr. and Mrs. Bloom today?"

My cheeks flush bright red, accompanied by a rush of mortifying embarrassment as it occurs to me that I'm staying in their house and yet didn't even know their family name.

His face twisted into an irritated scowl, the man waits for my answer, and so I say, "They've left for a few days—do you happen to know where they might have gone?"

He gives me a dismissive shrug in reply and turns back to his work.

Now that I'm standing up close to him, I can study his features a bit better and I notice that the left side of his face looks damaged. It's smooth and shiny, as if there had once been a now healed burn there, and on each side of his neck two small, straight white scars are visible.

"Would you like to join me inside?" I force myself to ask. "It's hot out here, and I really wouldn't mind some company."

He gives me an inscrutable look. "The Blooms don't want me in there," he replies, gesturing towards the house with his head.

It's obvious that he wants to be left alone, so I decide not to push my luck, saying only, "I'm sorry, I didn't catch your name . . ."

With furrowed eyebrows, he glares at the plants in the dented wheelbarrow for a few seconds.

"Alfred," he says finally.

❧

In the afternoon, I spend some more time in what has temporarily become my bedroom, studying the details dotted about the place.

On the wall, there's a heart-shaped wooden frame with "A+A" written in blue at its centre. I take it down from where it's hanging and hold it in the palm of my hand, studying the thick, flaking paint and the small dots all around the border. The piece of fabric used to hang it is slightly frayed, but somehow the plaque definitely stands out from the white wall and the rest of the room.

I spend some time wondering just who exactly those two letters might refer to. In a few short days here, I've met three people whose names begin with an A, so it could easily be any of them. Or it could even be something else—a symbol, for instance.

As I hang it back up in its place, a pang of hunger in my stomach makes me realise that it's almost dinnertime.

I walk in the usual direction, along the low hall that leads to the main part of the house, and once there, I turn on the oven and get ready to cook myself a proper meal. The clock ticks loudly as the time approaches 8:00 p.m.—but suddenly, that's no longer the only sound.

There's a person knocking at the door.

Remembering the growing number of nocturnal encounters I've had over the last few days, I soundlessly make my way over to the little foyer and lean forward to look through the peephole in the door; there doesn't seem to be anybody there on the other side.

Standing quietly, I wait by the door until I hear the knocking again. When it comes, I instantly fling the door open, removing the only thing keeping me and whoever is outside apart.

She's so tiny that I couldn't possibly have seen her from the peephole, but there she is, right in front of me—the same old lady who has been visiting.

What does she want from me?

"Why do you keep coming here?" I ask her impatiently.

With a defiant expression, she stares me straight in the face for a second—and then, seemingly gathering her strength, she screws her eyes shut and opens her mouth.

"You have to leave, now!" she shouts. "You have to leave, now!"

She shouts it again and again, over and over, each time looking more and more distressed until, after about the tenth repetition, she suddenly stops, turns on her heel, and leaves.

Completely dumbstruck, I just stand there with my mouth hanging open and watch her march back to the gate without another word.

The strong wind seems almost to be blowing her small body away, driving it off the property like so many dry old leaves, while I stand there speechless and watch her dissolve into the darkness.

DAY 6

AT LUNCHTIME the next day, I'm up and ready to go, but feeling too lethargic to cook a proper meal. Instead, I eat a chocolate bar that I find in one of the kitchen cupboards.

I continue to feel drawn to those huge windows in the living room, and find myself once again standing at them, staring at the shed. Nobody appears to be around today, and my interest in this odd outbuilding keeps growing.

Eager to give it a closer look, I hop through the open casement of one window and, still dressed in my pyjamas, walk barefoot across the grass.

I take a nervous peek round the rear and sides of the shed, but find nothing except stacked-up firewood and some piles of bricks, so I steel my nerve and take hold of the padlock hanging from a clasp on the wooden door.

Maybe I could force it?

No—Alfred would notice that right away.

Realising that it's not going to be possible, I give up on my idea of breaking into the shed and instead set about gathering as much information as possible about it from the outside. There are curtains over the windows, which make it hard to see inside properly, but peering around them as best I can, I could almost swear that I see something. *Is that—?*

"Are you finding it *very* interesting?" asks a voice, interrupting my reconnoitre.

I jump, terrified that Alfred has discovered me nosing around his shed, but to my great relief I see that it's actually Avery. He's standing over by the gate, a big smile on his face, laughing sweetly at my frightened expression.

I back away from the little wooden house and join him; he's wearing a striped white-and-navy T-shirt with matching dark-blue jogging bottoms, which makes me feel a bit less awkward about the way I probably look, lacking as I do either shoes or fresh breath.

I scratch my head and ask, "Do you happen to know the gardener?"

"Oh, yes. Alfred has something of a reputation around these parts," he says, as both of us look over at the shed. "You'd probably be wise to keep your distance from him."

"So, what are you doing out here?" I joke. "Were *you* spying on *me*?"

His eyes linger on my face for a moment, and his expression becomes serious.

"Yes—yes, I was," he says in a hammy voice, theatrically raising a hand to his brow. "You've found me out."

We both burst out laughing until he asks, "How is the house treating you?"

"What do you mean?" I reply, my laughter dwindling away.

"I've noticed lights on at night," he explains. "I was just wondering if you like it in there . . ."

Without wanting to go into it any more deeply, I give him a smirk. "So you actually *are* spying on me!"

He looks away, but for a split second I glimpse a sad look in his eyes, just like the other day. Worried that I might have taken the joke too far, I add, "The house is lovely—I'm just waiting for the owners to come back."

"Did they go away?" Avery gives me an enigmatic look. "If so, how is it that you're still here, then?"

I tell him about the day they invited me in and clarify that I'm only staying so I can thank them for their hospitality when they return.

He looks even more puzzled, to the point that he wonders aloud, "But if that's the only reason you're here, shouldn't you just leave them a note?"

Surprised that the thought has never even crossed my mind, I start hurriedly attempting to justify myself. "They were so kind to me, I really have to speak to them in person—I can't just leave."

"Is that the only reason?" he insists.

His questioning is starting to make me feel uncomfortable, so I lie. "I'm looking after the house for them." Not sure that he has fallen for it, I nervously fake a laugh and continue, "Actually, it's getting a bit chilly out here. I'd better get back inside."

He nods and lets me go with a vague half smile.

The truth is that I love this house, that there is something so homely and so safe about it, that even despite all the strange events, I wouldn't want to leave it. Ever.

☙

"Shhh—don't tell him I'm here," hisses the little girl from her hiding place between the armchair and the living room wall.

I gaze at her little form squeezed into that tiny space, wondering how I could have managed not to notice her arrival, and ask myself how long I've been sitting here, curled up on this sofa.

With a terrified look on her face, she brings her finger to her mouth and motions to me to keep quiet.

"*Him* who?" I ask, looking around me.

"The Derfla," she answers.

"The *Derfla*?" I repeat.

"He grows babies, and then he eats them," she blurts out, tears streaming down her face. "He's looking for me!" She suddenly covers her mouth with her hands. "He's coming!" she squeals, hastily pushing her way out from behind the chair and running down the corridor to my right.

I get up from the sofa to follow her, but for some reason can't get the lights to switch on, so I start carefully peering into every dark corner in an attempt to find her.

She isn't there, though—the only place left to look is my bedroom.

I slowly open the door, whispering that I'll protect her, that I'll help her, and that together we will fight this monster, but she doesn't reveal herself.

I place my cheek to the floor in order to have a look under the bed and I see them: two eyes, gleaming in the shadows.

I reach out my hand towards her, stretching farther and farther without any hesitation.

Until something grabs me.

Something strong—much stronger than any little girl could ever be.

I start screaming in fear

. . . and wake up, my face wet with tears.

I look around me. I'm on the sofa; the lights are on; there's nobody around.

It was another nightmare. Or was I hallucinating? Could that really be a possibility?

Plagued by the constant feeling that I'm being watched, I wrap the blanket around me and throw myself into bed, using the covers as a shield until I fall asleep.

DAY 7

AT 8:00 A.M., the alarm clock that I don't remember setting starts ringing, and has me up and ready for breakfast far earlier than the week's bizarre timetable has accustomed me to. It also reminds me that it's already been seven days since I first arrived here, and that what I'd imagined as a short stay has turned into something else.

As far as I know, I might well be staying here forever.

Amabel and Marvin still haven't shown up, the food is running low, and the weird events keep getting more and more unfathomable.

Through the window I see the gardener at work outside, face still set in that miserable frown of his, while these thoughts—almost undisturbed by his presence—rattle through my head.

I decide to make some coffee and take a cup out to him, but when I approach the herbaceous border he's tending, he acts as though I'm invisible.

"Hi there!" I say brightly.

He turns to glare at me briefly before lowering his eyes to the mug I'm carrying. When I hold it out to him, he grudgingly accepts it, and I sense that he might actually be lowering his guard—not much, perhaps, but maybe just enough for me to try to start a conversation. If this man is going to be one of few people—if not the *only* person—that I'm going to see while I stay at this house, I at least want our relationship to get off on the right foot.

As he raises the cup to his cracked lips, I stand there studying him a little more closely than strictly necessary, and suddenly my eyes widen in surprise: there's a dark red stain on his grey shirt.

Alfred notices my reaction before he's even taken his first sip of the hot coffee. He looks down at where I'm staring, then back up.

"It's from a plant," he assures me vaguely.

But the simple fact that he's bothered to provide me with an explanation brings two different, equally plausible ideas to mind:

1) He might be opening up to me.
2) He might be hiding something and feel the need to lie about it.

My reaction would be the same in either case, so I ask, "Can I get you anything else?"

He shakes his head and turns his back to me, so I take the opportunity to manoeuvre myself closer to the shed in the hope of getting a peek inside. Through the half-open door, I can vaguely make out objects scattered messily across the floor, but I want to see more—I need to. I move a step closer to the little cabin, but, somehow sensing my intention, Alfred immediately steps between me and the door and reaches behind himself to close it.

Feigning indifference, I give him a smile and back away silently until I'm inside my safe bubble again.

⁓

The day goes by, and I spend most of it spying on Alfred from the bathroom window; it's so small that I'm hardly visible from outside, and that makes it the perfect place for me to observe the gardener undisturbed, without him having the slightest clue what I'm up to—or at least, that's what I hope.

After yesterday's nightmare—if a nightmare is what it actually was—I can't rid myself of the thought that somebody is playing games with me. And I need to know if that person is the same one who's spending so much time in the back garden. I need to know if I'm safe or not.

Suddenly, Avery's words come back to me, reminding me to keep my distance from the man I'm now watching industriously pluck dead leaves from the foxgloves. But how can I, if I'm stuck here with him?

I don't know anything about him, and I need to find out more. And since Plan A—talking to him—has failed so miserably, I'll have to take another tack: observing him.

After a while, I leave my lookout post to get a snack and have a poke around for anything that might help me collect more information about this creepy gardener. A search of my bedroom doesn't turn up anything that might be useful, but when I open the drawer under the TV stand in the living room, I find a camera.

It's a cheap one, but it's in working order, and it has a full battery plus a memory card, as well as a video option.

I grab it and prop it up on the sill of the bathroom window, making sure that it's stable and won't fall into the bathtub and break. Once everything is ready, I press the Record button and leave it there, spying sneakily on Alfred for me, minute by minute.

My curiosity getting the upper hand over my nerves, I start preparing myself mentally to give the basement a more in-depth inspection than—for obvious reasons—I managed the other night. And I want to do it before it gets too dark.

Were those Alfred's feet that I saw just before I fainted? Is he behind all of this? New questions keep popping up inside my head, and if I want to answer them the only thing I can do right now is try to collect more clues.

With the camera now as my partner in crime, I don't feel guilty taking a few minutes off from my stakeout of Alfred to examine that underground room which I've only been in once—and in less-than-ideal circumstances.

Butterflies of anxiety are already starting to beat their wings in my stomach, but with my mind now firmly set upon the idea, I light a candle from the drawer full of them I find in the kitchen and, holding it steadily in my left hand, use my right to push open the cellar door. I make my way quickly down the stairs.

The atmosphere down here now is nothing like it was the other night; without all those candles, the light is different. The room is much darker, but somehow I don't sense any danger lurking within these stone walls.

There's a small wooden stepladder propped up against one wall, and the shelves and hooks dotted about host all the objects you might expect to find in a cellar: a toolbox, tins of rusty old screws, jam jars full of string and elastic bands . . .

I walk over towards the narrow, slot-like window set at the top of the wall, right where it meets the ceiling, and look outside: the fact that I'm underground means that the view from here is extremely restricted, and all I'm able to see is the front gate and the path—or at least a part of it. Even though it isn't much, I'm glad that I'm now aware of this space, particularly while I'm learning more about Alfred. It might help me gain an advantage over him and discover parts of the house that hopefully he doesn't know about. After all, he specifically told me that the Blooms didn't want him setting foot inside the place, so it's highly unlikely that he knows all of its secrets.

Somehow I've completely lost track of time while I've been down here—the only thing that tells me the minutes are actually passing is the hot wax dripping from my candle onto my hand and the floor.

The appetising perfume of what smells like a delicious dinner wafting in from somewhere makes me realise how hungry I am, and I set off towards the stairs with the intention of cooking myself a healthy meal—it's been a long time since I last had the pleasure of eating one—when suddenly my foot collides with something. It skids across the floor and hits the wall with a metallic clang.

I hold up my candle—it's the knife that I brought down

here the other night to defend myself with, for all the good it did.

I pick it up and climb back up the stairs to the ground floor of the house. But as soon as I reach the kitchen, I realise that something strange has happened.

I am not alone anymore.

A puff of air blows out my candle, and I drop it to the floor, race over to the dining table, and stand there, knife in hand, breathing heavily and gaping in disbelief at what I find before me: a banquet of appetising food—bowls of crisp, steaming vegetables; quiches; mashed potatoes and rutabagas with butter and pepper; pumpkin pie. It's obvious that at least one person must have been here to cook this, and that this isn't all just a strange dream.

But no one comes, no matter how long I wait.

Absolutely at a loss as to why all this is happening to me, it occurs to me for the first time that I might actually, seriously, be starting to lose my mind.

And right then, something even worse happens. Right before my eyes.

Hearing a tapping noise from the kitchen, I turn round, unable for a second to locate exactly where it's coming from. And then I do.

The fridge.

The magnetic letters on the chrome door are moving.

With spasmodic little jerks that grow more assured as I watch, a T begins making its way hesitantly towards an E. It's joined by a Y, which rattles as though fighting to free itself, and an instant later all the letters are twitching and shifting.

Slowly at first, then with increasingly decisive movements accompanied by delicate clicking, sliding sounds, they start skidding across the shiny surface of the fridge, gradually positioning themselves to form a sentence.

I watch, spellbound and horrified.

For you, dear Amethyst, it reads.

At this point, I'm seized by complete, total panic. I start trembling and spin round, searching desperately for anybody, anything, that might be making this happen.

But I'm the only one here.

Or at least, I'm the only *human being* here.

Terrified, I race over to the French windows in the hope of finding some sign that Avery is at home so I know that a chance exists of running away and finding somewhere safe . . . but outside, everything is pitch black.

It takes all of my courage, but I decide to turn off all the lights in the house and run as quickly as I possibly can into my bedroom, closing the door behind me and pulling the curtains shut across the window. Here, enshrouded in obscurity, is the only place I can still feel safe.

I lie awake in my bed for what seems like hours, unable to relax and jumping in fear at the slightest noise. At one point, I swear I can hear footsteps outside my door, followed by whispers, but I don't dare move an inch.

Most of the night passes like this, until finally the new day arrives and the first beams of morning light begin tentatively poking through the curtains of my window.

I haven't closed my eyes once, and my entire body feels achy and sore. I can say with some certainty that it's been the worst night I've ever suffered my way through in my entire life.

But despite everything that's gone on, despite all the bizarre things that I've seen, all the weird stuff that's happened, they still haven't managed to scare me off: I'm not going to run away.

I'm going to wait for the Blooms to come back.

And as the light forces the darkness away, my body and mind finally allow me to rest, and I sink into a deep sleep.

DAY 8

11:30 A.M. Time to get out of bed.

The air feels a lot colder than usual, and a strong wind is blowing impetuously against the house.

With a thrill of excitement, I remember the camera that I left filming on the bathroom windowsill the evening before and rush to retrieve it. In no time at all, I'm holding it in my hands and trying to find the video. The display says that it recorded for two hours and thirty minutes, only stopping when the memory card was full.

After giving the magnetic letters in the kitchen a couple of cautious pokes to make sure they're not going to start moving by themselves, I clear away the food from the table, covering the bowls with cling film and storing them away inside the fridge. Then I place the camera on the dining table, take a seat, press Play, and start watching.

For a good fifteen minutes there's no sign of anybody on the footage and everything appears to be completely normal—but when I get to the sixteenth minute, for a fraction of a second something changes slightly. I rewind and replay it.

In that brief instant, two events follow one another in rapid succession: the door of the shed opens, and random flashes of light appear, seemingly corrupting the footage. The next frame—like the following two hours—is a mixture of weird sounds and broken images. But not once does Alfred appear.

I think back to the previous evening—did I actually see him leave? Was he up to something in the house? Maybe his working day was over and he'd set off for home. But then what would have caused the camera to act this way? Is it possible that perhaps he spotted it through the window? And if he did, how did he manage to corrupt the footage without letting himself be seen even once? Or is it just a coincidence?

I feel more confused than ever, and the only thing that comes to mind is Avery's comment about the gardener, the warning to keep my distance. He obviously knows something about Alfred that I don't, and I need to figure out what it's all about.

After several days of wearing the same girly pyjamas, I finally slip back into my clothes, then brush my hair and splash my face with cold water.

I pause for a moment in front of the mirror to stare at a reflection that I'm slowly beginning to feel strangely disconnected from. The dark rings under my eyes are getting worse, and my lips are chapped, but what's most unsettling is the look on my face. Is this really me?

Trying not to let my appearance worry me any more than it already does, I walk away from the mirror, checking my breath in my cupped hand as I go: deadly.

In a half-hearted attempt to conceal it, I eat a yoghurt, too preoccupied now with getting out of the house as soon as possible to dedicate much thought to the problem of my halitosis, and soon afterwards I'm outside.

I squat down by the gateway at the back, somehow confident that Avery will turn up and stop to talk.

The wind blowing my hair all over the place, I wait. Without changing my mind. I have to stay here and wait for him. He's coming—I need to believe that.

After watching it struggle in the gusts of wind buffeting the earth, I rip a lonely daisy out of the ground and hold it between my hands.

The last few sunbeams which gave some warmth to the air are now departing, allowing the night to gradually take over the world.

At last, I hear his voice whisper, "Are you okay?"

Without wasting a single moment, I tuck the flower into my jacket sleeve and hoist myself up to my feet.

"I need to talk to you," I tell him as I brush my hands clean.

"Were you waiting for me?" he asks.

I nod in response, and continue. "The other day you told me to stay away from Alfred. Why?"

He casts a glance at the shed to make sure the gardener

isn't around, and then, his expression as serious as my own, begins to explain.

"There are rumours about him in this village."

"What kind of rumours?"

"Alfred has a past. Like all of us—except that his is pretty dark."

I let him go on.

"He moved to White Hills with his young wife about twenty years ago. They were newly married, they didn't have much in the way of money, so he started working as a gardener for some of the more well-off families in the village."

Intently, I follow his every word.

"Over the years, he gradually managed to put enough money aside to be able to afford a family home, on the top of that hill," he says, pointing at the highest peak visible beyond the cornfields.

"I don't see it," I cut in. "Where do you mean, exactly?" But he ignores my question.

"At that time," he goes on, "his wife, Lilly, was pregnant. The day she gave birth, Alfred took a day off to be with her. The next day, he turned up for work, and he looked—a mess. Completely done in."

"What happened?" I whisper.

Without taking his eyes from mine, he continues.

"Lilly had died in childbirth." Avery lowers his eyes. "Then, two days after—after the tragic event, Alfred went missing. People started looking all over town for him, in all the local pubs. But there was no sign of hide nor hair of him anywhere."

As he speaks, I file each word away in my memory.

"Later that night, his house was set on fire."

My eyes widen as I listen to the end of the story.

"By the time the fire brigade managed to get the blaze under control, the house was completely devastated. The police investigation found the babies in their cots . . . but it was too late to save them," he concludes.

Twins.

"What about Alfred?" I ask.

"The next day he showed up in the village with a burn across his face—and that was proof enough for some people that it was he who'd done it," he replies.

"Did he confess?"

"No, he never said a word about it. The police questioned him, but he was never charged with anything. People in White Hills started to believe that he'd killed his sons, though. Because he thought they'd caused Lilly's death."

He pauses for a moment before adding, "And that's when all the grown-ups started telling kids scary stories about the Derfla, so they wouldn't go out wandering the streets at night."

"The Derfla!" I burst out, shocked by this last part of the story.

Confused by my reaction, he shoots me a funny look and then picks up his story again.

"The people round here were convinced that Alfred was a murderer, so right away they started trying to force him out of his job and out of local social life. Pretty much everyone just started ignoring him, acting like he wasn't there at all. And they used a backwards version of his name—Derfla—to try to . . . well, connect him with evil. Make him into a kind of a monster, I suppose."

Another piece of my puzzle clicks into place, and so I

ask, "If that's what people say about him, how come he's still working for the Blooms?"

"The Blooms, they're nice people," he says with a shrug. "Mr. Bloom didn't want to give up on Alfred, so he allowed him to stay on in the shed in exchange for working on the property. That went on for quite a while, until one day Mrs. Bloom accused him of stealing a picture from the house."

"A picture? Why on earth would he do that?"

"Mr. Bloom's theory was that someone was trying to set Alfred up—someone who wanted him out of the village for good."

"How do you know all of this?" I ask, brushing away the lock of hair tickling my nose.

He smiles. "Well, I grew up in that house," he says, gesturing with his head to the huge grey edifice behind him. "So obviously, I got to hear all the stories about my neighbourhood. And anyway, on the day of the fight about the picture—the one Mrs. Bloom accused him of stealing—I was out playing in the garden and I could hear all the shouting."

I burst out laughing, and the atmosphere suddenly turns awkward.

"What do you find so funny?" he asks coolly.

"The fact that you've apparently *always* had a thing for spying on people," I say with a chuckle.

He frowns dismissively—but then a rueful smirk appears on his face, and it's not long before he's laughing softly too.

The wind gathers strength, so I pull my jacket tighter around me for extra warmth. Ready now to get back inside, we exchange polite goodbye smiles and head off towards our respective front doors.

After just a few steps, though, I turn again and say out loud, "Do you believe he really did it?"

He takes a few moments to gather his thoughts and then turns towards me with a pensive expression on his face.

"I don't know, if I'm honest . . ."

He shakes his head.

"But I wouldn't take any chances."

DAY 9

I OPEN MY eyes at the creak of my bedroom door opening, but continue feigning sleep while I listen to light footsteps which cross the parquet, stumble against the chair by the desk, and let out a soft gasp of surprise.

I'm lying with my face turned the other way, so I can't see who it is, but I'm not afraid. In fact, I almost feel like I know who's sneaking about in the room: the young girl from my dreams.

Is that who it is?

I sense movement near the wardrobe, as if the person is trying to quietly open it. Too curious to wait another second,

I suddenly sit bolt upright in bed and look in front of me.

I was right—it's her again.

"What are you doing in my room?" she asks, surprised to see me appear from under the blankets.

"Is this *your* room?"

She nods, adding, "You need to leave. If you don't, he'll find me."

"The Derfla? Is he still after you?" I whisper.

Obviously terrified by the sound of that name, she starts trembling and nods again, her frightened eyes searching the room.

"Why do you think he's looking for you?"

"Because he created me," she explains, as though stating the obvious. "And now it's—it's time for him to *eat* me."

I can't hold back my amusement at this childlike logic. It's like when children who should know better let themselves get so worked up about the Bogeyman that they actually start to believe he exists. Her words provoke an involuntary giggle from me, but it's obvious straightaway that my reaction has upset her, so I put on a serious face and ask, "What makes you think he *created* you?"

"Because—because I don't have any parents," she replies.

"What do you mean?" I say, genuinely taken aback. "Why do you say that?"

"Because I don't!" she shouts.

☙❧

Another dream.

What is this mystery all about? Is Alfred the gardener the man that scares her so much, or is it just the idea of this monster that all the village kids are frightened of? Most importantly, who *is* this girl who keeps appearing to me? Does she need my help? Is she actually in danger?

Hoping to come across some crucial clue that I might have missed, I mentally run over my conversation with Avery.

According to the story he told me, Alfred had twin boys—there was no mention of any girls. And the girl said this bedroom belonged to her, but if that's the case, where is she now? Where is she in real life, I mean—outside of my nightmares?

My eye falls upon the heart on the wall.

A+A.

Might that be a clue?

If I ever want to get a good night's sleep in this house, I'm going to have to figure this mystery out, once and for all.

I'm going to have to help her.

❧

It's five thirty in the morning, and I've spent the last two hours huddled up under the covers running my brain ragged, trying to work out if there's some kind of logic linking all these different events. But for the life of me, I can't—too many pieces of the puzzle are missing.

The new day's sun is starting to make its appearance, lighting up the white walls, and although I've hardly slept at all, it's a clear enough sign that it's time for me to get up and get busy.

I shuffle tiredly to the bathroom, where I take a quick shower and clean my teeth. As I brush, I look at my reflection in the mirror, and my concerns about my appearance return: I'm losing weight, my skin looks dull, and my cheeks are sunken. My hair is all messy and tangled, and my skin is getting paler and paler by the day, making me look absolutely exhausted—I almost look like I've seen a ghost.

Ready now to head outside, I'm walking towards the front door when a thunderingly loud noise reaches my ears. I gaze up at the ceiling, wondering suddenly if this house has another floor of which I am not aware. From what I've been able to make out, there aren't any corridors or doors that might lead to an upper level—but then again, I haven't really had time to investigate every inch of the house.

Standing inches away from the corridor, with my hand still grasping the doorknob, it suddenly occurs to me that I've never checked out the Blooms' bedroom—it's right at the end of this corridor, between the bathroom and the basement.

I turn around and walk back down the hall until I'm standing in front of the door.

It feels strange, as though I'm about to cross an invisible line.

I twist the handle and push, and the interior of their room is revealed: a luminous, airy space, beautifully decorated in the same style as the one where I'm sleeping, but much, much brighter. To the left, a large French window looks out over the side of the garden I haven't yet had a chance to visit, while the centre of the room is dominated by an imposing four-poster bed with cream-coloured curtains. Over on the right, a very old wooden wardrobe completes the furnishings.

I walk over to the large French doors that open to the garden and study the space outside. A small fountain stands in the middle of a gravelled space which seems to be cut off from the garden proper. All around it, a neatly trimmed square-cut hedge delineates the margin of what would appear to be Amabel and Marvin's special little corner. Two wonderfully intricate white iron chairs are placed next to the water fountain, separated slightly by a small table between them.

Tempted to go outside, I grasp the key and am on the verge of turning it in the lock when all of a sudden I hear that *noise* again.

I spin round in alarm to check if there's anybody there.

Nothing.

I peer about nervously for a couple of seconds, then decide that I should probably turn my attention to the ceiling. Set in the white coffered panelling is a small square hatch with a cord hanging from one corner. I position myself directly underneath it and jump up, trying to reach the cord, but a few failed attempts later, I give up in frustration.

As I look up at it, I suddenly remember the stepladder that I noticed in the basement the other day, and so, with pulse racing, I find myself once again walking down those dark, rickety stairs.

When I reach the bottom, I see what I'm looking for, still propped up against the far wall. Cheered by the thought that I won't have to spend too long down there, I stride across the stone flags and take hold of the ladder—only to find, a few seconds later, that hauling it back up the stairs is unexpectedly difficult.

After a few less-than-successful attempts, inspiration strikes, and I lay the ladder flat upon the treads of the steps and slide it upwards until it bumps into the bathroom door, at which point I clamber past it and haul it up from the top, leaning it against the corridor wall.

Glowing with pride at the success of my efforts, I carry it into the bedroom and position it right under the entrance to the attic.

Compared to the struggle of getting it here, actually *climbing* the ladder turns out to be a piece of cake: I can feel the reassuring support of its steps beneath my feet until I'm high enough to grab the cord and pull down on it with all of my might, and the panel swings down, revealing a dark opening.

The stepladder wobbles but doesn't tip over, allowing me to continue my ascent and make my way into the unknown space above.

Inside, it's cramped and gloomy—what feeble illumination there is comes from the little bull's-eye window of coloured glass in the pediment, but it's nothing like enough to be able to see clearly.

However, after I've been up there a few minutes, my eyes finally start getting accustomed to the low light, and what at first had seemed to be nothing more than an awful lot of blurred shapes start to resolve into something a bit clearer.

I look around me, taking in the various strange symbols that are dotted all over the place, covering practically every inch of the walls. There are piles of old books collecting dust, all seemingly related to religious topics, to judge from their titles.

Part of me is none too surprised to see all of this—every house hides some secret or other of its owners, after all. But I'm starting to feel worryingly as though I'm embroiled in something sinister—something that I might have been wiser not to get involved in at all.

Crawling farther into the small space, I stop to look at a framed photograph that I find propped on a chest, showing five people posing for the photographer. I pick it up and, as best I can, clean away the dust.

Under my right thumb, the Blooms, probably still in their forties, are smiling cheerfully at the camera. Marvin is wearing the same round glasses and a collared sweater and is hand in hand with Amabel, whose dress is as pretty as her freshly done hair. On the opposite side stand a younger couple. They could almost be the Blooms' grown-up children, if it weren't for the fact that they are visibly of different ethnicities: the man at the edge of the frame is tall and serious and appears to be Caucasian, but his face looks nothing like those of the Blooms, while the girl he has his arms around is clearly Asian. There's a sad look in her eyes, but she has a sweet face. She's left her straight black hair loose and is wearing a long, flowery dress for the event.

Her attention is not directed towards the camera—in fact, she's the only one who isn't holding a pose. Instead, her head is tilted downwards towards where a little girl—*the* little girl—is standing, smiling with her eyes closed, holding both Amabel's and the other woman's hands, right in the middle of the picture.

She looks much younger than she's appeared to me in my dreams, but I'm 100 percent certain that it's her.

I turn the photo over in the hope of finding a date or a name or something, but whatever was written on the back has been scribbled out and is now impossible to read.

I place the frame back where I found it and turn my attention to studying the chest itself: it's safely fastened shut by a heavy padlock hanging from a hasp on the front. I look around me for a key that might open it and spy a bunch of them hanging from a nail under a painting on the wall. I snatch it down and, one by one, try each of them—but none works.

Tired and frustrated, I decide that the time has come to take a break and get some fresh air.

I climb down the ladder, pushing the small panel shut

behind me, then walk down the corridor and back into the main part of the house.

The sudden chiming of the clock makes me start, and I realise how long I've spent up there—it's 11:00 p.m.

It was still morning when I found the door to the attic—is it really possible that I've spent the whole day in that room without realising it? It's true that while I was up there I had no way of knowing what time it was, but it seems pretty unlikely that I could have spent so much of my day inside that pokey, dusty place.

No reasonable explanation presenting itself, I slip back into my pyjamas, hop into bed, and focus on the fact that I'm finally on the right path—now, I have a lead to follow.

Despite not feeling drowsy at all, I keep my eyelids firmly shut and try to force myself to fall asleep in the hope of having another of those dreams, but it's no use—my mind is far too restless and doesn't calm down enough to let me relax properly until hours later.

Exhausted by the thoughts racing non-stop through my head, I eventually let go of everything and drift off to join the dream world.

DAY 10

MY DISAPPOINTMENT at not having dreamt about the little girl gradually fading, I lie there on my side with my eyes closed and let the rays of light shining through the window caress my cheeks—until the sky starts clouding over and the sunbeams disappear, depriving me of the warmth I'd been enjoying so much.

I open my eyes, only to see Alfred's dour face peering in at me through the window—but as soon as he notices my alarmed expression, he vanishes from sight.

Why was he staring at me? Has he been doing it all this

time? Is he trying to scare me? If that *is* what he's trying to do, he's definitely succeeding.

With a growing feeling of paranoia, I tug the curtains shut and change into my regular clothes.

While I eat some cereal for breakfast I try to come up with a plan of action. I have to confront him, this creepy, cantankerous gardener. But I have to be smart about it too. I can't let him know that I'm afraid, or—even worse—that I've been spying on him.

I make a mental list of my options and pick the safest: I'll ask him about the Blooms and hint that I know about his past. That should get me some answers, and at the same time make him realise that I'm not afraid of him and know that he's up to something.

To give myself a pretext for starting the conversation, I make some coffee. I walk across the lawn towards him, holding it out and not saying a word, but he refuses it with a disdainful wave of his hand.

Right. That makes things harder.

But, undeterred and determined to show that I'm not intimidated by his grouchiness, I casually take a sip of it myself. "Rough night?" I venture, noticing the tired look on his unshaven face.

"Rough life," he replies with deadly seriousness, avoiding eye contact and busying himself with running a pair of garden shears over a whetstone with assured strokes.

Taken off guard for a moment by the blunt nonchalance of his answer, I spy an opening.

"You do spend a lot of time working on this garden."

He still doesn't look up at me, so I go on.

"Is it your way of repaying the Blooms?"

Even though his face is turned away from me, I can tell from the way his jaw muscles tighten that he's gritting his teeth.

"Is sticking your nose into other people's business *your* way of repaying them?" he replies, without raising his head from his work.

Now completely off my guard, I back away from him and gather my thoughts. I try to figure out a comeback, but before I can come up with anything, he starts talking in a husky voice.

"Reverend Bloom was always nice to me. Helping him with his garden is the least I can do," he says, apparently sincerely. "You ought to be grateful too," he adds.

"I am," I burst out.

Reverend? The word starts bouncing about inside my head.

"Well, make sure he knows it, then," he says, squatting down to look at his precious delphiniums.

But what on earth is he referring to? How does he know that the reason I'm still here is to thank the Blooms for their hospitality?

Suddenly, there's a rattling noise and an amber vial of medication falls out of one of Alfred's pockets onto the bright green grass, where it lies, label upwards.

Sleeping pills.

That's *it*. The clue I've been waiting for.

It really *might* be he who's behind all of the strange things that have been happening—I have the proof!

No more words come out of my mouth—or out of Alfred's, predictably—so I withdraw indoors. But the thick walls and locked doors can't keep away a growing feeling of fear. I'm besieged by a multitude of worrying possibilities which make my head spin and my stomach ache, and I'm starting to feel nauseous.

Sitting myself down on the arm of the sofa, I grab some paper and a pen from one of the shelves of the bookcase and start quickly jotting down all the impressions and facts that I've gathered over the last ten days:

1) The Blooms are nowhere to be found.
2) During my first few days here, a strange old woman kept insisting that I had to leave the house.
3) I've been having recurring nightmares whose protagonist is a little girl who claims to be afraid of something called "the Derfla."
4) Alfred, the gardener, has been acting oddly and seems to be hiding a secret.
5) Thanks to Avery, my neighbour, I've been able to learn more about the events in Alfred's past which gave rise to the legend of the Derfla in the first place.
6) My conversation with Avery also proved to me that I didn't just dream up the Derfla, that it's something local adults use to scare children into behaving themselves.

What connects all of these things?

I'm so close, yet so far away from discovering the one piece of the jigsaw puzzle that I need. I can't give up now.

Here's my theory, for what it's worth: since the Blooms' disappearance, the only person that I've come across on the property is Alfred, who is always distant and standoffish. Is it possible that both the elderly woman and the young girl in my dreams have been trying to warn me about something awful that's going to happen? Is it possible that Alfred the gardener has done something to Marvin and Amabel?

And is there even the smallest chance that he's been playing games with me in order to eventually get rid of me?

In my mind, the answer is clear.

☙

I raise my eyes from the floorboards I've been staring at blankly for the last hour and take a look outside. It's only early afternoon, but the sun is already starting to sink in the sky in preparation for disappearing behind the hills.

I spend a good fifteen minutes hanging around by the window, just to make sure that Alfred isn't about. There being no sign of him in the back garden, I head for the corridor in the direction of the cellar to be certain that he's gone away for the day—I can get a decent view of the gate from there.

I'm creeping down the hallway as quietly as I can when I hear a sound coming from downstairs.

And as soon as I do, my breath freezes in my mouth.

"It's too risky," a female voice whispers. "We need to wait, as we discussed."

I fling open the door and walk through it, but as I expected, there's nobody to be seen. Certain that someone must be hiding somewhere within these walls, I close the door behind me, leaving myself in complete darkness, and run down the stairs to the centre of the room.

The frightening things that happened during my first visit down here are at the forefront of my thoughts, but I try to push those memories away and focus on the here and now.

If Alfred actually is the person who is playing games with me, he could have been drugging me all this time. All the voices, all the weird events might only be in my mind, and I've got no way of separating what's real from what isn't. The only thing that I must make sure of is that he isn't able to get close to me when I'm not looking. I have to be completely vigilant at all times and never let my guard down.

The problem is that's a lot easier said than done.

Checking on the gate through the small cellar window, I see Alfred trimming the bushes along the sides of the pathway. I stay put and wait for him to finish, not missing a single one of his movements, until he stalks out of my field of vision and forces me to find another spot from which to observe him.

Once I've climbed back up to the ground floor, I decide I'll turn off all the lights to try to make him think that I'm not home, then immediately afterwards find myself a good hiding place that still allows me to observe his every move. I crouch behind the old sofa so I have a clear view through the big French windows while still remaining hidden—if needed, I can also walk over to the door to spy on him through the peephole without being spotted, obtaining a view over two sides of the house.

I stay huddled up like that for hours, until I feel my body aching and my eyelids starting to droop.

DAY 11

THE CLOCK strikes 3:00 a.m., and the sound of its chimes makes me jump. I must have fallen asleep for a few hours. But I can't go to bed now—I have to stay awake.

I'm lying on the floor, unsure what I should do next. Twisting my head around, I check that I'm alone.

Alfred doesn't seem to be about, so I stand up and start looking for a flashlight to help me find my way in the darkness. I hunt through every drawer in the living room and kitchen without luck before remembering the candle that I dropped on the floor in shock a few nights ago. I carefully make my way through the gloom to the corridor and am pleased to see the candle still lying where I left it. I pick it up and use a match from the box by the stove to light it.

At the same moment, a light comes on across the back garden.

It's coming from Avery's house.

I stand there in silence, staring out at that lonely window which glows with such bright light—light which after my prolonged stay in complete blackness looks a lot brighter to me than it actually is.

My heart starts beating faster. Not because I'm worried or scared, but because I'm *glad* to see that light in the darkness. It's comforting, somehow. It makes me feel safer.

Framed by the neighbour's window, I see the movement of a silhouette which stops dead at its centre, as though looking right at me.

Is it Avery? Can he see me?

Around the house everything seems quiet, and the air is unnaturally still, so I put on my shoes and head outside, hoping he'll notice me. But it's not until I've turned the two corners of the house that I realize Avery is no longer by his window—he's already walking to meet me by the gate.

Instantly, I feel a smile forming on my face, and I blush at the thought that I'm so pleased to see him.

"How did you—?" I start to say, but before I can finish my sentence, he breaks in.

"I saw you coming out."

My smile gets wider—which, considering the situation, makes me feel a bit silly. For a moment I just stand there looking at him. His usually messy hair looks even more tangled than normal, suggesting that he probably just woke up. He's somehow managing to look cute anyway, though.

Then I see the sweatshirt he's wearing. Across the chest in giant capital letters is the word "FLAWLESS," and at the sight of it I can't hold back a dorky guffaw.

He looks down at the source of my amusement, and then back up at me.

"What, you mean you don't agree?" he asks, feigning perplexity.

We both laugh, and I start to relax a little bit.

"I'm glad you saw me coming out," I confess.

There's a moment of charged silence between us, which he breaks with another question. "So how is it that you're awake?"

I consider not telling him the truth, to try to make myself sound a bit less pathetic, but then decide that it'd be better to open up and be honest.

"I can't sleep. I have a . . . weird feeling."

"What do you mean?" he asks kindly.

"I keep . . . hearing things," I admit. "And seeing people. In the house."

"And does that keep you up?" he says, seemingly unruffled by my words.

"No," I say. "I have to stay awake. I *need* to."

"Maybe you should try to get some sleep instead. It might just be that you're overtired."

"Never mind," I answer, irked by his hint that it might all be in my head. "Forget it." I turn quickly on my heel and start walking off.

"Wait," he says, raising his voice, "that's not what I meant."

"Then what *did* you mean?" I ask sharply, without turning back round to face him.

"I mean . . . that it's hard," he explains. "Being on your own for a long time. I know how it feels."

Repenting, I walk back to the gate and look him in the eyes, feeling an urgent need for him to understand me.

"I'm not imagining things."

"I know," he whispers back, without breaking eye contact.

We stare at each other, and it's clear that we are both feeling something—there's a connection between us.

Still speaking in a low voice, I tell him, "I don't know if I'm safe here."

His eyes shift to the dark bulk of the house behind me.

"What *exactly* is it that you're afraid of?" he asks, his expression becoming more intent.

"I have this feeling that won't go away. The sensation that I'm being watched, constantly . . . and I'm afraid that the person behind it all is Alfred."

I immediately realize how silly I must sound, but it's too late to take it back.

"I can stay out here and check that nothing weird happens," he offers, suddenly every inch the solicitous young gentleman. "If you feel like you're in danger, you can always come over and find me. I won't leave."

Overwhelmed by his kindness, I move nearer to him, reaching the limit of the gate between our gardens. We're so close that I can almost feel the warmth of his body next to mine.

"I can't let you stay out here alone, though," I say, after the silence has drawn itself out for a few instants.

"Oh, I don't mind," he reassures me.

I consider his offer, and then a thought pops into my head.

"Tell you what—we could *both* spend the night out here, until the sun comes up. But I wouldn't want you to feel that you have to . . ."

"Sure," he answers, without hesitation.

And so just like that, we find ourselves sitting with our backs propped against the two sides of the gate. The only thing illuminating our surroundings is the gently flickering candle that sits in a little pool of its own hardened wax on one of the stones of the path.

I can hear him breathing, in and out, and the rhythm of it soothes me to the point that I close my eyes and start to sleep.

When I wake up, it takes me a few moments to work out where I am. I turn around to check if Avery is still there and, disappointed to find that he's not, I get up from the ground and brush my hands clean on my jeans.

"Hey!" shouts a voice from behind me.

Somehow I manage to spin around in time to catch the apple that's flying through the air towards me.

There he is—Avery, walking this way through the dewy grass, another apple in his hand.

"I did *tell* you that I wouldn't leave you," he says, with a wide smile on his face. "Nice catch, by the way!"

I return his smile and thank him for the apple, and he takes a bite from his.

"You seemed pretty concerned last night," he says as soon as he has finished chewing. "Would you like to talk about it?"

I reflect for a second and try to straighten out my thoughts, then, finally, let it all out.

"Maybe . . . maybe I'm crazy, but I'm starting to think that Alfred might be drugging me," I say. "All the things that I see, all the weird things that have been happening to me . . . I can't explain it, and it just feels natural to blame all of this on him."

"Why would he do that, though? I mean, what possible

motive could he have? Have you thought about that?" he asks.

"Well, I know that this will sound ridiculous, but I'm scared he might be up to something big."

"Like what?"

"Like, where are the Blooms? You said it yourself—Mrs. Bloom didn't like the idea of having him around."

"So what exactly are you saying?" he asks, sounding intrigued.

"I don't know what I'm saying," I admit. "I just . . . I don't know. That's why I'm not sleeping. I need to keep my eye on him."

"I understand," he says affectionately, "but don't forget to take a break and catch your breath sometimes."

I just nod.

"In any case," he adds, "if you ever need me, you know where to find me."

Still not entirely convinced that he's taking my fears seriously, but grateful in any case to have him on my side, I thank him, and for a short, intense moment we stand facing one another over the gate, me wishing that I didn't have to ever let him go away. But I realize we both have things to do, so I politely say goodbye and make my way back inside, in desperate need of a hot bath.

※

As I walk towards the front door I pick up the newspapers and magazines again lying on the doorstep and, once inside, dump them unceremoniously on top of the stack accumulating on the console table.

One of the newspapers slips to the floor and falls open to a page of adverts for local businesses and events. I run my eyes over them—it's the usual assortment of provincial weirdness:

The Hills Inn Line Dance and Barbecue—Live music from Hank Akeley and the Black Mountain Boys . . .

Wilma Nightmoth, Psychic and Seer—Not a fraud!!! Since 1954—drop in at 13 Chapel Lane and speak to the dear departed . . .

LOST!! TIBBLES—Our lovely cat, black-and-grey coat, one leg missing. If you see him, please call . . .

White Hills Hardware, Est. 1890—A knife for every occasion! . . .

Machen and Sons, Greengrocers—Special offer: pumpkins half price (while stocks last) . . .

I reach down, pick it up, and fold it closed, and as I do, the words on the front page catch my eye. The headline is in bold capitals and reads "TRAGEDY ON CHURCH ROAD," and there's a photograph of a broken body, its face covered with a sheet, lying on the ground surrounded by a crowd of onlookers and some ambulance staff. The fields in the background of the picture are easily recognisable as the ones in front of the Blooms' home, or at least ones very much like them, and I feel certain that the accident must have taken place somewhere around here.

I place the paper back on top of the others and go to finally take that much-needed bath.

As soon as the water in the tub is hot enough and the steam has started misting up the mirror on the wall, I take off my clothes, dump them on the white wicker chair in the corner by the sink, sit on the edge of the tub, and slowly lower my feet one at a time into the scalding bathwater, sliding the rest of my body in as soon as I've got accustomed to the temperature.

A feeling of extreme relaxation starts to suffuse my entire

body, and thoughts of the night that I've just spent in the garden with Avery come vividly back to me—it's probably the only positive experience I've had since my arrival here, other than that of living in what I would consider my dream house.

As I remember the moment that passed between us before I fell asleep next to him, I feel my cheeks warm with a blush.

Is this what infatuation feels like? Have I ever even *been* in *love*? So many things about my own past seem blurred and inaccessible in my mind, to the point that I can't even answer my own questions about myself.

At that moment, my train of thought is interrupted by the sound of the keyhole cover being moved, as though somebody is trying to get in.

I leap out of the bath, struggling to keep from slipping on the wet floor as I cross the room, and place my hand on the doorknob, waiting. Maybe I'm just being paranoid, as I don't hear anything else, but needing to be sure, I twist the handle.

And, to my horror, realise that I'm locked inside.

I'm certain that *I* didn't lock the door—I've never even seen a key for this room, and there was certainly none in the lock. I can feel a sense of dread mounting inside me.

With my composure beginning to crumble, I start anxiously shouting, then banging and eventually kicking at the door, yelling for someone to let me out.

But nobody does, and my panic is getting closer and closer to being pure hysteria. My heart is beating so fast that it feels as though it's about to explode, while the air in the room gets thinner and thinner until I can scarcely breathe anymore.

Finally, I collapse onto the cold marble floor.

DAY 12

SLOWLY, MY senses start to return, and I carefully get myself up from the bathroom floor.

There's no longer any light shining through the window, which suggests that it must now be night-time outside. I reach for the doorknob, hoping with all my heart that it'll turn and let me out—and to my surprise and relief, it does.

Without wasting any time, I pick up my clothes, wrap a towel hurriedly around myself, and run down the hall towards the living room.

When I get there I pause for a moment, looking about me and trying to work out what it is that has happened. I peer into the kitchen and see the digits of the clock on the stove click over to 2:00 a.m.

Hiding myself as best I can from any prying eyes, I put my clothes back on and dump the towel on the clean kitchen table. I open the fridge and find some fresh fruit—which I'd swear I hadn't noticed in there before—but only take out a bottle of water to hydrate myself. Feeling my wobbly legs begging me for mercy, I pull out a chair from under the table and sit myself down.

And then I see the camera that I left there a few days back.

I turn it on and replay the long clip, stopping at the fifteenth minute. As expected, the glitch at the sixteenth minute is still there, and so I replay it over and over again, watching as closely as I possibly can and studying every tiny detail.

Eventually, I manage to pause and capture a frame that I haven't noticed before: right after the shed door opens, a strange light is visible coming from it for a split second, and I can barely believe my eyes when I realise that I'm looking at a face in there.

I zoom in on the picture, focusing on the shape of the light: as the image increases in size it starts to lose clarity, but I'm still able to make out some features that I recognise—it's Alfred's expression, beyond a doubt. Just somehow a bit warped.

But what does this mean? That he's a ghost? A demon? Has he actually *become* the monster that keeps the Derfla legend alive?

If that's the case, I need to prove it.

I look behind me, over at the fridge—the plastic letters

that scared me so much the other night are still there, still spelling out the same words. Could it actually have been *him* who wrote that? But why would he write "dear" if he doesn't even know me? It doesn't make any sense . . .

But maybe it doesn't really need to make any sense.

I stand up and touch the letters, sliding them into different positions until a new sentence appears.

Who are you? the row of letters across the fridge now crookedly asks.

I step back, waiting.

Nothing happens. Could it be my presence in the kitchen that's stopping the supernatural forces from showing their hand?

Avery's words come to mind again—"Take a break and catch your breath."

So I follow his advice, leave the room, and lie down on my bed, listening to the sound of my own deep breathing until I feel so relaxed that I drift off into a nap.

☙❧

My eyes open again to the sound of thunder rumbling in the distance.

Feeling pleasantly rested, I decide immediately to check if my question has been answered. I walk down the corridor towards the kitchen and the fridge, but nothing has changed, and I tell myself disappointedly that there's only one thing left to do: break into the shed and get it over with.

My blood's up now, so I grab a large knife from the wooden knife block by the sink and head outside.

I open the front door, only to be almost forced back inside the house, so strong is the wind that's blowing out there. But I push my way through it, struggling to keep walking until I've turned the first corner, where the wall shelters me just a little bit from the crazed weather.

The distant thunder is rapidly moving closer and closer, bringing freezing-cold rain with it, and in just a few seconds I find myself soaking wet instead of bone dry.

But I can't go back: I won't be satisfied until I've found out what the hell is inside the damned shed.

I cross the back garden and arrive in front of the shed. After a moment's hesitation, I raise my knife and start prying at the thick chain around the padlock and the hasp on the lock, but they're far too solid for it to be any use.

I take off my jacket, wrap it a few times around my right fist, and give one of the tiny windows to the side of the door a good punch—it shatters into thousands of fragments which scatter all over the place, and I put my arm through the hole I've created, feeling about with my hand for anything that might help me open the door.

My fingers touch on various useless odds and ends, until finally they come across something flat, sharp, and cold. I slide my fingers along it until they encounter a wooden handle—an axe! Just what I need!

I wrap my hand around it tightly and start pulling it upwards, in the direction of the window: it's heavy, but I've almost got it.

And then, suddenly, a violent freezing sensation grips my whole body and for one horrifying second leaves me completely immobile, unable even to move my eyes—and then sends me crashing heavily to the wet ground.

Barely conscious, I feel warm tears make their way across my cheeks as I lie there on the grass in the icy rain.

I can't move, I have no control over my body, and I'm scared. But none of that really matters.

One thought—one thought alone—keeps going through my mind.

I am going to die here.

DAY 13

I DON'T KNOW how much time I spend there, alone, frozen to the ground, before I pass out.

The only thing that I do know is that I am now waking up to mild, calm weather. I'm very uncomfortable—but I'm *alive*.

And I'm glad about that.

I have absolutely no idea what happened. Or why. I can't get my head around it. Perhaps I ought to try to just put it behind me. Forget about it. And maybe learn not to act so irresponsibly.

The only explanation that I can come up with is that Alfred must have found me looking too closely at his precious shed and decided to do something about it. I don't know how he could have paralysed me like that, and I've no way of confirming my assumption, as I didn't see or hear anybody near me when I fell to the ground—but I do know that it's the only thing that would make any sense at this point.

"Are you okay?"

A distant, concerned voice reaches my ears, catching me off guard.

"I . . . I don't know," I mumble, still lying on the damp lawn. Silence.

"Are you okay?!" the voice repeats, louder this time.

It takes me a moment longer than it probably should before my brain finally makes the connection that it's Avery's voice I'm hearing.

"Yes," I answer, "I . . . just need a second."

I collect my strength and sit up straight, turning in his direction. He's by the gate, wearing a white T-shirt which sets off his neatly combed dark hair. He looks smarter, more dressed up than usual. Is he going somewhere?

Obviously quite worried, he smiles with relief as soon as he sees me look him in the face.

Running a hand through my uncombed hair, I suddenly realise with a pang of self-consciousness how I must look, but—trying to conceal my embarrassment—I say bluntly, "I was attacked."

His eyes widen. "By who?"

"I have no idea—I didn't see anybody."

"So what happened, then?" he says urgently.

"I was trying to get into the shed, but something stopped me," I explain. "My body was paralysed until I passed out."

"Amethyst," he says, his face suddenly growing dark, "this

stuff sounds serious—you shouldn't be staying in that house."

From the intensity in his voice I can tell that he cares about me, and it gives me a nice warm feeling inside, but I can't take his advice—not this time.

I shake my head, not taking my eyes from his.

"Why on earth are you so stubborn?" he continues, with audible frustration. "You're always the same."

He closes his mouth hurriedly, as though that last sentence had just slipped out unintentionally.

"You don't know me," I say, frowning. "How can you say something like that about me?"

From his expression I can tell that he realises how much he's upset me.

"I'm sorry, I didn't mean that," he apologizes, his voice soft now, and his affection for me shining through.

"I'm sorry too. But you have to understand—I *can't* leave. Not just yet. What kind of person would I be if I just walked away from this, turning my back on the people who have been the nicest to me?"

At my words, his face lights up as though he actually, finally understands, and that makes me feel better, and gives me the confidence to continue.

"By the way," I ask, "do you happen to know the girl who used to live here?"

Upon hearing my question, Avery's face darkens again, and his eyes grow shiny as though he were about to cry.

"I'm sorry," I blurt out in concern, "I shouldn't have asked . . ."

"Oh, don't worry. It's fine," he tells me as he struggles to regain his composure. "Yes, I know her."

"What's her name?" I ask.

"Akiko," he replies, as though the question were a ridiculous one. "We grew up together."

"How old is she?"

"She would be nineteen years old," he answers, looking upset by my questions and clearly fighting back tears. "Why are you asking me this?"

"Where is she now?" I manage to ask at last.

"She . . . she died. Recently."

And just like that, a tear steaks down his left cheek to quickly hide itself at the corner of his mouth.

"I'm sorry to hear that," I say, meaning it.

The sight of such raw emotion holds me back me from asking anything else. I just stand there next to him, hoping that my presence is enough to comfort him in some way. I'd like to hug him, to let him know that it's not just him who's there for me—that I'm there for him as well. But I feel too guilty about having made him cry to come out with a sudden show of affection now, so I stay where I am, waiting for him to calm down.

He dries his eyes with his forearm and flashes me a gentle smile, which immediately cheers me up.

"Thank you," he says, taking me by surprise.

"For what?" I say, confused.

"I'd been needing to get that out . . . and you helped me to do it. So thank you."

I smile too, relieved to hear that I'm not actually as awful a human being as I'd started to think.

"Would you like to join me for dinner?" I venture.

He looks tempted by my offer, and moves his hand forward as if he is about to take mine, but instead he stops halfway and rests it on the wooden gate.

"I don't think that's a good idea," he replies.

I go bright red, wishing I could take back my invitation and avoid having created this awkwardness. I'm lost for words, but luckily he knows what to say.

"We could have a picnic, though?"

"Isn't it a bit too cold for a picnic?"

"Not if you bring lots of blankets!" he responds cheerfully.

❦

We agree to meet at 7:00 p.m. by the gate and both bring some food and things to drink. Excitedly, I walk back inside the house and start preparing some simple dishes for us to enjoy. On the menu: toasted bread and smoked asparagus. I'm about to take some candles from the drawer where I found the others, but it occurs to me that it makes things a bit weird if I try too hard to create an atmosphere, and so I leave them on the countertop.

Next, I take a long shower and dry and brush my hair into place for the first time.

I put back on my dirty clothes—which quickly spoil all my efforts at making myself look presentable—and as soon as the clock strikes seven I pick up the dishes I've prepared and make my way outside.

When I reach the back garden, I'm happy to see that the gate between the two houses is open and a red-and-white-checked blanket has been laid neatly on the ground. There's a basket placed in the middle of it, and I can see the hot steam from the food Avery has cooked rising up into the evening air, giving off a delicious smell. He hasn't seen me walking towards him yet, busy as he is with his efforts to light a small tealight, but once he hears me coming he jumps up and invites me to take a seat.

We're sitting facing one another across the threshold between our respective gardens, but I feel incredibly happy that the physical barrier which was keeping us apart has been removed.

And without further ado, we tuck in to a thoroughly enjoyable meal, devouring every last morsel of the dishes we have prepared, from the appetizers of toasted bread and sliced salami, which are as simple as they are delicious, to the home-made chocolate pudding that Avery produces as a dessert.

As I run my finger round a plate to collect the last few crumbs, I become conscious of how late it has got. The sky is dark, the first few stars have come out, and the cold air is making my nose tingle.

Even though I'm freezing cold, our being here together like this more than compensates for the fact. But when he notices me shivering, Avery says, "We should probably get going—it's pretty late, you know."

Secretly wishing that he hadn't spoken those words, I nod and reluctantly get up and start gathering the crockery and cutlery to take back to the house. Before I can leave, though, he says, "It was nice to spend some time with you."

I simply nod my head mutely up and down to let him know I feel the same way.

"If you ever feel lonely, or you just want some company," he continues, "flick the lights in the house on and off a few times, and I'll show up out here. You don't have to be alone."

"Is this your way of letting me know that you're *still* spying on me?" I smirk, and we both laugh.

"Maybe," he says, with a wink.

I wish him goodnight and leave, happy to have spent an entire day with him.

DAY 14

I'S THE middle of the night, but someone is knocking repeatedly on the front
door. I ignore it at first, but then start
wondering if maybe there's the slightest chance that it's Avery
who's standing out there.

I leave the lights off while I walk down the dark corridor
I am by now so accustomed to until I approach the source of
the sound.

Knock . . .

Knock . . .

Knock.

The noise is slow, yet loud, and so eerie that I daren't get too close to its source. It goes on and on for several minutes. And suddenly, the unexpected happens.

The doorknob starts turning by itself, warning me that whoever was wanting to attract my attention is now going to get it.

The hinges creak eerily as the door gradually opens and a tiny hand appears around it, followed by the rest of the body to which it's attached.

It's the old lady—the one who keeps appearing and pointing at me.

And I don't like where this is going one bit.

As I'm backing away, I trip over the leg of the sofa and fall to the floor.

I crawl backwards, trying to put as much distance as possible between us, but I can't get away from her. Floating jerkily through the air, like a plastic bag blown by the wind, she gets closer and closer to me until I can feel her cold breath on my neck.

"I warned you," she says, staring at me. "I warned you. Now you are going to be stuck in here for all eternity."

I squeeze my eyes shut as hard as I can, repeating to myself that it isn't actually happening, that it *isn't real*—but then I feel her wizened hand harshly grab my wrist.

"You can leave with me now," she says.

"Or you can rot in here forever."

⊘⁄⊚

When I open my eyes I'm in bed, drenched with sweat, my forehead burning. Was that a dream? It felt so real, yet so dreamlike. So . . . *other*, as if I had been in some different dimension.

I pull my arm out from under the blanket, revealing the red marks on my wrist. I have no idea exactly what it was, but it definitely wasn't just a nightmare.

☙

I'm awake, and I've got a strong feeling that something is wrong.

I check the clock: 11:35 in the morning. Everything's quiet.

Too quiet. No wind, no birds singing, no noises.

I make myself some porridge, unable to shake the thought that somehow, something is different. Something has changed.

I place my breakfast, along with a glass of water, on the table and sit down to enjoy it. As I take a sip, I wonder to myself what Avery is doing. Is he still sleeping? Is he having breakfast, like me? Is he studying? Or maybe playing video games?

All of a sudden, something more important crosses my mind: where's Alfred? I can't allow myself to lose track of him at any time, and I haven't been doing such a great job of it— my mind has been somewhere else entirely for far too long. It's been days since I last saw him. Has he gone away? Time passes so quickly that I can barely even remember when I last spied on him, but I can't erase the image of his twisted, ugly face on the camera footage—just thinking about it makes me shudder.

Annoyed with myself about the underwhelming progress of my investigation, I take the spoon out of my mouth, stand up, and walk over to the French windows in order to take a good look at the back garden. The grass is freshly cut, and everything is as pretty as ever, but something looks different. I just can't spot what it is yet.

I scan every inch of the area, certain that I'm right, and then I notice it: the door of the shed is just a little bit ajar.

It's the first time it's not been locked. And it's my only chance to finally take a good look inside it.

Without wasting any time, I rush over to the front door and pull it open. A gust of wind shoves back at me. I look up and see the huge, dark cloud which is about to completely cover the sky.

I step back inside, grab my jacket, and run back out, hoping that if I'm quick I'll manage to avoid the rain. In less than a minute I'm by the shed, my heart racing. After what happened when I tried to break in the other day, I've developed an irrational—or maybe not so irrational—fear of that little wooden hut in the garden, but I can't let that stop me now.

I try to be brave, grab hold of the handle, and slowly open the door.

From the old wooden floor, my eyes move quickly upwards until I find myself looking at the most shocking thing I've witnessed in my entire life.

Alfred is hanging there, a rope running from his neck to one of the beams of the shed roof.

He's flailing about, struggling madly to stay alive, his purple lips looking almost as contorted as those of the face I saw in the film.

His horrified eyes meet mine.

It takes a second for me to understand what's happening in front of me and to snap out of my state of shock. I grab hold of his body to try to give him some support while with one hand I grope for the old chair to my left and slide it under his feet, allowing him to stand up and release his neck from the noose that is strangling him. As soon as he's freed himself, he collapses down into the chair, breathing heavily and avoiding any eye contact.

I sit on the floor in front of him, waiting for an explanation, too upset and astonished to say anything.

A long pause anticipates his words.

"Why did you do that?"

"Why did I save your life?" I reply, irritated.

"Why did you bother *helping* me?" he says.

"What was I supposed to do?" I ask, unable to help raising my voice, "let you die?!"

"You should have," he says flatly, ashamedly honest.

Both sitting there inside the place that I'd so much wanted to see, we let the silence prevail.

⁂

It's getting dark, and I'm still sitting here in a corner of the shed, waiting for some answers. I don't say a word, but we both know that he'll *have* to talk sooner or later—neither of us will leave until he does. And I have all the time in the world.

It takes a few hours, but in the end he finally decides to acknowledge my existence and enlighten me about his motives.

"I thought I was dead," he says out of nowhere.

"Yeah, well, you very nearly were," I snap.

"No. I mean before," he insists. "Before you came."

"I know. But I *saved* you."

"You don't get it. I'm not talking about today."

"Then what *are* you talking about?" I ask.

"A long time ago. I killed myself," he confesses. "Or at least, I thought I did."

"And then what happened?" I say, staring at that face whose eyes are still avoiding mine.

"You," he says, this time turning his face so I can clearly see his despondent expression.

I feel cold and hot at the same time, suddenly frightened of what's about to come.

"The day you came to this house, I saw you," he continues, "and you saw me."

"What do you mean?" I say, confused.

"After what I did to myself . . . after I'd committed suicide, nobody ever talked to me. I was invisible. And so I'd always supposed I was dead."

"But *I* saw you," I say, starting to understand what he's getting at.

"And not only that. You talked to me—so that must mean that I'm alive, mustn't it?" he says, almost as confused as I am.

I take a moment to ponder, but without finding an answer.

"I would guess so," I tell him, and reach over to poke at his knee. "I can touch you—you're as real as anybody else to me."

"Then how do you explain the fact that I can't die?" he asks. "I've tried to kill myself dozens of times since you arrived here: suffocation, hanging"—his eyes rise for a second to the cord hanging from the rafter—"I've tried all kinds of different things, but nothing seems to work. . . . *You* can still *see* me. And it's driving me crazy."

I immediately remember the pills that fell from his pocket, his constant bad mood, and that footage—could it be that I'm able to see him even *though* he's a ghost? I can't take any chances, though: I have to make sure I know what I'm working with.

I tell him to sit still there and wait for me, and I run inside through the pouring rain. The camera is still on the table where I left it, so I snatch it up and, sheltering it from the rain with my body, hurry back round to Alfred. Before going into the shed I turn it on, empty the memory, and hit the Record button, then push open the door with my shoulder and point the camera directly at his face. He looks at me with a puzzled expression, but when he realises that I have a plan he gazes trustingly into the lens.

I let the camera film for about thirty seconds, when it suddenly slips from my wet fingers and falls to the floor. I pick it back up, quickly checking for scratches to the body or the lens, but it looks fine. Relieved, I stop recording and play the clip back.

Nervous to discover what the footage will tell us, I sit myself down next to Alfred and, with a shaky index finger, press Play.

The screen shows the door opening, and then just an empty shed. Absolutely not a human soul appears, not even for a moment. When the clip hits the twentieth second, I pause it, having seen enough.

That confirms it, then—Alfred is indeed dead.

But one word keeps popping into my mind.

How?

I look at him, then at the footage, and I can see no logical or plausible connection between the two. How can this be happening? How is it possible? How am I able to see him?

Pushing against the bubble of confusion that seems to be engulfing me, I ask myself what Alfred must be feeling: he doesn't want this life, yet he's stuck here. With *me*. Why am I the only one who can see him?

Abruptly, a thought strikes me. Is Avery able to see Alfred, too? I remember our conversation about him, about the legend of the Derfla and the fact that he didn't want me to get too close to the gardener—but why would he say that if he knew that Alfred was already dead? And how could he *not* know about Alfred's death, considering how much he knows about everything else?

Is he hiding something from me?

I suddenly feel as though I can't trust anyone but myself, and at the thought I get a feeling like a stomach cramp that makes me feel strangely nauseous and dizzy—so dizzy, in fact, that I start to stagger, and Alfred immediately jumps up, grabs my arm, and helps lower me down to the dirty shed floor between the piles of chipped plant pots and tins of weedkiller.

My vision is blurring, growing darker and dimmer by the second, and the only thing I can hear is Alfred's voice telling me to breathe deeply.

And then I pass out.

DAY 15

WHEN I come back to my senses it's way past midnight. Alfred is still next to me in the shed, waiting patiently for me to sit up. He's holding out a glass of water.

Seeing him like this, I would never have guessed that he was a ghost.

Wait a minute—if he really *is* a ghost, how come he can *hold* things?

I reach for the glass and grasp it steadily in my right hand, looking at the water trembling in time with my own shivers. As he steadies my head so that I can drink, I can't help but compare this Alfred to the one that I'd previously met: he's acting so differently, perhaps relieved by the fact that he doesn't have to hide from me anymore.

"So how did it happen?" I ask when I'm feeling better.

"What would you like to know, exactly?"

"Everything," I say, a determined look in my eyes.

He pauses for an instant, and then begins, haltingly, to tell his tale.

"It happened nine years ago. It was the seventeenth of August. I remember that it was a really hot day, the temperature was well above the average. Damned hot. I'd taken a day off to stay with Lilly, my beautiful wife. She was in labour, you see. She was only twenty-seven years old, and I was thirty at the time.

"It was supposed to be a special day, that day—the beginning of our family. And then later I was told the—the sad news by our trusted doctor."

He pauses for a moment.

"The . . . *bright* side of the story was that I had two wonderful newborns, twins. Seth and Benjamin, we'd decided to call them. I took them back to the house, put them in the nursery that we'd done out. Well, it was Lilly who'd done it out, really.

"I remember going into their room and watching them sleep. They were all that I had left. The morning after, I went to Lilly's hometown to start organising the funeral. And when I got back that night, the person that I'd got in to look after Seth and Benjamin had gone. And so had my house. And my two kids . . ."

His watery eyes show the agonised emotions that reliving these events is stirring up in him.

"I'm sorry," I manage.

"People in the village started to blame me for it all," he continues. "They started calling me all kinds of awful names, until they came up with the worst one of all—'the Derfla.'"

For a moment he stops fiddling nervously with the knotted piece of garden twine in his hands, as though his feelings are too much for him to handle. I keep quiet and wait until he's ready to speak again.

"I lost all my clients, one after the other, until I was working exclusively for the Bloom family. Reverend Bloom was the only one convinced that I'd been set up, that it wasn't my fault. That I'd never have done anything like that to my own kids. Didn't matter that the police had investigated me, didn't matter that they'd cleared my name. Other than him, nobody else believed it."

He takes a deep breath before continuing.

"But that was enough for me. I was just grateful to have someone on my side, especially somebody as influential as Mr. Bloom was. But then the practical jokes began . . ."

"Like the picture," I interrupt him.

"Like the picture," he confirms with a nod.

"People wouldn't look at me in the street. They'd just . . . just completely ignore me. And the kids! The kids would scream every time they saw me, run away from me. It was awful. In the end, I couldn't take it anymore. I managed to keep going for four years, and then, five years ago, I decided to end it all," he concludes.

"And you've spent all of the last five years here?" I ask, curious about what happened.

"Yes. I've never left the garden. And I've never gone into the house. I spend all of my time here. This shed has become my home," he answers.

"Why the shed? Why not another place?"

"I've come to believe that there are two reasons for that: the first, which is the most obvious, is that I don't actually have a home anymore. And the second . . . The second is because this is where I took my own life," he confesses, casting his eyes upwards at the wooden joist from which the rope still hangs.

"So you're *stuck* in here?" I ask.

"That's one way of putting it. But even if I *could* go anywhere else, I wouldn't leave. I don't have anywhere else to go," he says, brushing away a tear with the back of his leathery hand.

Another question forms in my mind.

"Don't ghosts usually cross over, or something like that? Don't you want to leave this place once and for all?"

"I wouldn't mind that, but I can't leave," he says.

"Why not? What's keeping you here?" I insist.

"The Blooms were the only ones who were nice to me, and I let them down—I disappointed them. The least I can do is to keep doing what I promised I'd do," he says, sounding a little bit too much like me for comfort.

"Don't you think they would want you to find peace?" I ask.

"I can't know that for sure. I *have* to stay here and do my job," he replies, as though he has no choice in the matter.

"I'll help you," I offer.

But—suddenly switching back to the rude brute he was when I first met him—Alfred replies scornfully, "I don't need your help."

❧

I lie on my bed looking up at the pretty ceiling. I wonder why Avery never mentioned Alfred's death. Is he really unaware of it? But he knows so much about everything else, how could he not know about *that*?

Beginning to feel upset, as though suddenly certain that he's lying, I walk to the living room, where the clock tells me that it's now 10:24 in the evening. I turn the light on and off repeatedly, as Avery told me to do if I needed to talk to him.

A split second later, the lonely window in the tower of his house, which I can only imagine belongs to his bedroom, comes on in answer, signalling his presence.

I find my shoes and make my way round to the gate. It's dark. I have no flashlight or candle to help light my way, and the wind blowing through the trees in the blackness makes the atmosphere sinister, but as I walk I trail one hand along the wall to guide me, and after the usual double left turn, I see the gate.

Avery isn't there yet, so I wait impatiently for his arrival.

I spot him walking down the stairs of his front porch, but he doesn't see me straightaway. When he reaches the gate, there's a concerned look on his face, probably due to the urgency of my call, but he also flashes me a brief smile—that is, until he notices my serious expression. He looks at me questioningly.

"Did you tell me *everything* about Alfred?" I begin.

"Yes," he answers, looking perplexed. "Why?"

"Do you know what happened to him?"

"I told you his story," he says, seemingly sensing what's about to come.

"No, I mean after that."

"Would you mind being less mysterious?" he asks, mild irritation at the turn our conversation is taking beginning to creep into his voice.

"Did you know that he died?" I ask finally.

He pauses for a moment, as though picking his next words carefully.

"Yes. Five years ago," he admits.

My jaw drops in disappointed shock at his admission. "Why didn't you tell me that before?" I ask. "How could you have left that out? And more importantly, why did you bother telling me to stay away from him, if you knew he wasn't even really here?"

"Isn't he?" he counters.

My eyes widen with the realisation that Avery might know a lot more than he lets on. Does he know I can see Alfred? Is he able to see him as well? I have to know, but all I manage to mumble in reply is, "I don't know, is he?"

Looking disappointed by my attitude, he says no more, so I seize the opportunity to ask another question.

"Can you see him?"

He doesn't answer. He just gives an evasive shrug, which makes me think there's a chance that, like me, he can.

By this time he's looking quite upset. So much so that he starts backing slowly away from me. When I notice, I press him.

"Why can't you be honest with me? I know you don't owe me anything, but you could at least *try* to help me."

The hurt and desperation evident in this last sentence seem to cut through his emotional fragility, and he looks me straight in the eyes and says, "We shouldn't be talking about this."

"Something is going on in this house, and I can't ignore it, Avery!" I tell him. "Maybe that's how you're used to living your life, just watching everything without doing anything about it—but I'm not like that."

Realizing how nasty I must sound, I open my mouth to apologize—but it's too late. Avery has turned his back on me and is walking away without uttering a single word. Tears start welling up in my eyes as I stand there by the gate, trying to control all of my confused emotions.

Finally, they force their way out as silent sobs.

DAY 16

A T 9:20 the next morning I open the door of my bedroom and walk out into the long hall. I feel tired and awful, but I know I can't hide in bed forever.

Shuffling like a zombie, I make my way to the kitchen, where I pick up one of the few remaining chocolate bars and take it with me into the living room. I sit there apathetically on the sofa, letting time pass by without me and staring out the windows in the hope of seeing Avery, tormented by yesterday's spat.

I know I was in the wrong. I know there was no justification at all for me behaving like that towards him, and that there's absolutely no excuse for the things I said. I don't know much about him, after all, yet even though we were complete strangers until a week or so ago, he has repeatedly been there for me.

I look around the room, feeling an urge to keep myself busy so I can avoid dwelling on Avery too much, and find something that works perfectly: almost hidden away up in the top corner of the bookshelf, I spy the book that Marvin was reading the day we met—*Spiritual Relief.*

I toss my snack onto the coffee table, walk over to the bookcase, and jump as high as I can in an effort to reach it. But it's no use, so I drag over a chair from the dining table and climb up on top of that.

My fingertips brush against the black leather binding of the book, and I slide it out from the shelf where it belongs. It's not a big volume, but it feels heavy, and by the look of it I can tell that it's pretty old. Inside the front cover, the blue title appears again at the centre of the flyleaf, followed by the authoress's name—Vivien Bisset—and the date it was written, 1948.

Turning it over, I find a list of the book's contents: the various chapters, all dealing with spirits, divide the book into sections.

The first chapter is called "Know the Spirit." I flick to the page and read the sections into which it is divided: "Rudiments," "Ghosts," and "Spectres."

A quick skim through "Rudiments" reveals that there are different types of spirits with which we may come into contact during our lives. Some might be ghosts, some might be spectres, but in between these two categories are numerous other subtypes, each differing from the others.

The book explains that when you come across a spirit, your awareness of its existence means that it notices you as well—until that specific moment, it may not have been aware of your presence at all. Acknowledging each other's existence is the first step to take in order to understand which type of spirit you are dealing with.

The page goes on to explain all of the various types, so I skim through it in search of a category that might fit Alfred's case. When I reach the word "suicidal," I stop dead in my tracks.

The paragraph describes how spirits who have died a terrible death—caused, for example, by murder or suicide—should be considered dangerous, as they may be haunting the location in which they passed away, and their frustration at being stuck there and having to re-experience their death over and over again may result in constant anger and cause the ghost to be unwilling to collaborate.

After the list of all the various other kinds of spirits, a new chapter called "Signs of Haunting" begins, describing all of the various things which might occur when one encounters a spirit. But, already fairly certain now of what Alfred's situation is, I decide to skip over it.

The third chapter, titled "Select your Spirit," is where the authoress explains how a more-than-expected number of spirits might be gravitating towards the same area. Some may be aware of the others in their environs, while some may not be conscious of one another's presence, their level of awareness being lower.

A little confused by this last piece of information, I flick forward a few pages and find a section titled "Awareness" where Ms. Bisset talks about how some spirits, depending upon the circumstances of their deaths, may become aware of their situation, while others might remain completely clueless. In both cases, they may either cross over directly or find themselves stuck in a certain place or with a specific person. And for this very reason, it's vitally important to be able to connect with the spirit you want to help or get rid of without bothering the other ghosts which might be in the same location but unaware of their surroundings.

The book also underlines how important it is to be extremely careful when talking to a ghost, as it may well be ignorant of the fact that it has ceased to be alive (as in cases of sudden or unexpected death)—and in the rare case that you do upset it, it might react violently.

I skip some more pages and reach chapter six, which is titled "Talk to the Spirit." As Alfred didn't seem too keen to talk to *me*, this part might come in handy, but I decide to jump forward to chapter ten, the last in the book, titled "How to Help." Here, the writer gives an exhaustive description of how to assist spirits in crossing over, depending upon their story and type.

After running over Alfred's case in my mind, I jot down a list of important points about him, following Ms. Bisset's indications:

1) Ghost
2) Non-malevolent
3) Suicidal
4) Aware of his situation
5) Unwilling to collaborate

Now that I have a better understanding and a clearer definition of what type of spirit Alfred is, I can search for the section of the chapter that will tell me what to do.

When I eventually find it, I'm relieved to discover that there is a solution. The authoress writes that good ghosts with a sad past might be holding onto the world of the living as a personal punishment, as if the pain they had suffered in life wasn't enough and they needed it to continue after their death. Unable to find peace, they are usually unwilling to listen, which makes it harder to help them.

She explains that the only way for them to let go is to be certain that they have been forgiven and accepted by the people they hurt during their lives.

I slam the book shut.

So that's what Alfred needs in order to cross over—he has to realize that he *has* been forgiven. But forgiven by *who*, exactly? His family? *They* knew he wasn't a bad person.

Maybe the reason he's stuck here is because of this ludicrous story of the Derfla—he isn't able to forgive himself for it, even though it was other people's judgement rather than his that brought it about. He just has to realize that he needn't keep blaming himself for it.

But how? How can he forgive himself if people won't believe his story?

Or maybe—just maybe—that's *it*. I have to open people's minds and show them the real picture. I have to make them understand once and for all what actually happened, so that they can finally forgive Alfred and let him rest in peace.

Before putting the book away, I open it at the middle part and read some more, in particular a chapter which explains how ghosts that have spent a long time in the human world after their deaths might begin to gather strength, and how a ghost that is unaware of its death might act and feel the same way as any regular person.

Overwhelmed by all this new information, I flick through the pages until I reach the last, which reads:

This shall not be considered as a complete spirit guide. All the information provided in this book derives from my own personal experiences with the paranormal. I shall not be held responsible for any eventual unfortunate events.

☙

By night-time I feel confident that I've got the answer I was looking for.

I grab a bite to eat and head outside in search of Alfred. I tread the same path I am starting to know so well, crossing the back garden and ending up at the shed. I knock gently and push the unlocked door open.

He's sitting there on the floor, looking extremely miserable.

When I enter, he doesn't bother to stand or even look up, but that doesn't really matter to me: I'm going to help him, no matter what.

I join him on the floor, sitting fairly close but at the same time leaving a bit of distance between us. And I begin.

"You said you paid someone to look after the children that day . . ."

He nods slowly.

"Did she die in the fire?" I ask.

"They didn't find her body," he replies obliquely, confirming what I had already suspected.

"Have you ever heard from her since the accident?" I wonder.

"No, she just . . . disappeared."

"How come you asked *her*?" I ask. "Was it somebody you already knew?"

His eyes lock suddenly onto mine, as though trying to tell me that, yes, he *did*, but without wanting to say it out loud.

"It was somebody you cared about . . ." I whisper.

"Yes," he says, raising his voice, "yes, it was—but it's not what you think."

"Then tell me," I say gently.

He pauses, lost in thought for a few moments.

"It was my sister. My little sister," he admits finally. "I knew about her . . . *condition*. I wasn't thinking straight. She'd been fine for years. Even so, I knew deep down that it wasn't a good idea to leave her alone with the babies, but I wanted to trust her. After everything I'd been through, after what had happened to Lilly—I *needed* to trust her."

Tears start to stream down from the corners of his eyes.

Aware that I risk crossing a line, I steel myself and ask, "What do you think happened to her?"

"I don't know. I abandoned her, and she disappeared. I failed her. I failed Lilly and my kids. I failed everybody."

It occurs me that the situation is suddenly more complicated than I'd been expecting. What am I supposed to do? How will I be able to get this man to forgive himself? Even if I could get his sister to talk to him, what would that change?

Unsure about what step to take next, I ask just one more question.

"What about your scar?"

He touches it lightly with his fingers and says, "I got it when I helped her run away."

Lying on my bed, I'm having no luck at getting my mind to switch off. I can't just give up on him; I have to figure out a way to help. But how?

How . . . That's what this is all about, finding the answer to that one simple question.

I check the clock, which is now telling me that it's 11:59, but I can't get to sleep and so I get up to do something that, in the middle of the night, I probably shouldn't.

DAY 17

12:01. ONE specific thought keeps going round in my mind: are Marvin and Amabel aware of Alfred's presence so close to their home? Mr. Bloom was reading that book by Vivien Bisset, which suggests that he might indeed be aware of the fact. But then, why disappear? Did they leave—or did something happen to them?

Unable to provide myself with any kind of satisfactory explanation, I sneak out of the room and, leaving all the lights off, venture through the corridors of the house. When I reach the entrance to the cellar, I stop and listen, placing my ear against the wooden door: all quiet.

I walk on and twist the handle of the door to the master bedroom: even in complete darkness, the room is still as cosy as it is when the sun is shining through the French windows. I'm not sure what it is I'm searching for, but I have a strong feeling that this is where I'm supposed to be right now. To find something.

I start looking around, beginning with the pretty dressing table on my left—nothing useful there—before moving my attention to the bedside tables.

I don't find anything interesting in the first one, but luckily enough the second contains a chunky flashlight.

I reach for it, give it a shake, and then push the switch. A beam of light appears: it works.

As I'm standing right next to the bed, it seems logical to crawl underneath and see what I find, so I do. There's a box hidden there. I grab it, slide it out, and silently open it.

I sit the flashlight on the floor with its beam pointing upwards like a lantern, and it illuminates my surroundings enough to allow me to see what I'm holding: a photo album. I undo the ribbon which fastens the front and back covers of it together and open it at the first page.

At the centre are the handwritten words "Our Family," followed by the date—1996.

I turn it over, revealing a large picture set in the middle of the next page. Marvin and Amabel are at the sides of the frame, while the little girl—Akiko—is in the middle, blowing out a candle on top of a cake which is shaped like the number four.

A new page, this time containing numerous smaller pictures. I give them a brief looking over and realise that the Blooms must have adopted Akiko when she was young, probably from the other couple I saw in the picture a few days ago.

Is that the reason why in my dream she said that she didn't have any parents? Did she know that the Blooms weren't her natural parents? She was so young—how could she have worked that out?

I wonder why those other people—her birth parents—couldn't keep her. But I'm sure the young couple had their reasons. You could tell from the looks on their faces.

Still leafing through all these happy pictures, I hear footsteps behind me and I turn my head, bracing myself for the sight of somebody. But I'm a split second too slow to see if there's anybody there or not—by the time I've snatched up the flashlight, whoever was sneaking up on me an instant ago isn't there anymore.

With the feeling that I'm being watched, I close the album, place it carefully in the box, and slide it back where I found it.

Flashlight in hand, I leave the room, close the door, and go back to my own bedroom.

I open the drawers of the desk, searching for anything that I might be able to use to make sure the door of my room stays shut. Inside the second one on the right I find a baby-pink ribbon—perfect.

I wrap it around the handle of the door, then around the mounting of the lamp attached to the wall over the bed—one of those reading ones—and tie a double knot, thinking that although a pretty pink ribbon is certainly not the ideal way to keep people out, it's still better than nothing.

When I start feeling calmer, I spend a minute reflecting. The book I was reading explained that there may well be more than one ghost in any one place. Is it possible that Mr. Bloom didn't know about Alfred? Is there a chance that the reason he was studying that book was actually somebody *else*?

This last question brings to mind a vital detail that I'd completely forgotten: Akiko, the Blooms' adopted daughter—and recently deceased, according to Avery.

Is that the reason why Mr. Bloom has the book?

Things might be starting to become clearer.

At the same time, Ms. Bisset's words also make me wonder if there are perhaps other spirits in addition to Alfred haunting this place—that would explain all the uncanny noises and weird things that have been happening. Maybe, just maybe, even the elderly lady who is so obsessed with me might have passed away and is confusing me with somebody else she cared about.

Feeling suddenly overwhelmed by all these hypotheses, I change into my pyjamas and climb under the covers, hugging them tightly to me.

෴

A raven clattering against the bedroom window wakes me up.

Still half asleep, I pull away the blanket and make a quick trip to the bathroom where I wash my face with cold water, brush my teeth and hair, and study my appearance. Nothing's really improved since last week—I still look as exhausted and undernourished as before, but I try not to let myself get too self-conscious about it and to stay focused on more important things.

Before leaving the room, I peek through the small window, curious as to whether Alfred is already at work. Yes, there he is, raking some dead leaves from the ground, unaware of me staring at him. I leave the bathroom and make my way to the kitchen, where I prepare some more porridge and a glass of milk for breakfast, then slowly make my way towards the living room, with not one but two things simultaneously on my mind: first, of course, Alfred, and second, *Spiritual Relief.*

Are there any other books about spirits in this house, I wonder? The shelves are stuffed with dozens of tomes on subjects related to religion, but are there any others like the one by Vivien Bisset that are mostly focused on ghosts?

I scan the titles in front of me, but nothing catches my eye, so instead I drag over the same chair and reach up for the same book once again, hoping to find some more useful information that I might have missed the first time I looked at it—after all, I did skip over plenty.

I quickly turn the pages until I see chapter seven—"The Matter of Time"—and I sit down on the sofa and pick my way through it carefully. I learn how the perception of time is vastly different after death and can vary according to a variety of factors, but is generally either faster or slower than normal. Apparently, the lack of any regular perception of time is directly related to the lack of a physical body, which means not being affected by time changes as we experience them while alive.

The book also explains that ghosts don't exist in a specific place at any given moment, and in fact a spirit might well jump into another dimension for a period of time—which can vary—without realizing it. Completely unaware of what has happened, once it gets back it will resume whatever activity it was performing before the point of detachment.

I redirect my attention over to the window just in time to notice the shed door opening and Alfred emerging. I'm observing the gardener's movements when my attention is captured by the copse of imposing, twisted trees right down at the very end of the garden. *How I could possibly have missed noticing them before?* I ask myself.

I ponder the question for a few moments until it suddenly strikes me that I've lost track of Alfred, so I rush over to the French windows and hurriedly locate him. There he is, trimming the grass around the gate to Avery's house and stealing a glance in my direction every now and again. Does he want to talk to me? Is this his vague way of trying to get my attention?

Mindful of the wet weather, I collect my shoes, together with an umbrella, and walk out into the back garden.

Before I have a chance to open my mouth, though, Alfred marches straight up to me and asks, "When you said you would help me"—he pauses for a second, studying my expression—"did you mean it?"

"Of course," I reply, confident of my abilities.

A fog is beginning to settle on the garden.

"How?" he asks, his eyes full of hope.

The tension is becoming palpable.

"Let's go inside," I suggest, "and I can explain it to you there."

With Alfred at my heels, I make my way to the shed, closing the door once we're inside. He stands there, anxious to know if I really have an answer to give him—the answer that he wants to hear—and so I begin.

"I've found a book, and it's helping me understand the situation."

Alfred only nods vaguely.

"I'm learning a lot, but I need your cooperation," I tell him, staring at his pallid face.

"What do you need me to do?" he asks, bracing himself for my answer.

"I just need to get to know you," I say at last.

When we are both sitting on the rough wooden floor, I start asking him personal questions, trying to understand exactly *which* of my hypotheses about what's keeping him here is the correct one, and he opens up completely to me in a way I'd never have expected. Gratified by his frankness, I listen carefully to what he says, paying attention to each small detail of his troubled life, until finally he reveals the thing that I've been dying to hear.

"I worked hard to be able to afford to live in this village. I did everything I could, and I managed it. As an *honest man.* Now all that's left of me is that damned *legend.* It's unfair— just totally unfair." He grits his teeth. "How am I supposed to join my family, who've been waiting for me for all this time, when I can't prove to them that I'm deserving?"

I gaze at the knots in the floorboards, trying to work out what he means, but can come up with nothing to dispel my doubts. So instead of answering his question, I ask a new one.

"You obviously love your family. Why are you so sure that that's not enough for them?"

Out of nowhere, he suddenly leans forward, grabs hold of my shoulders tightly with his strong hands, and shakes me.

"I failed them once before!" he blurts out despairingly. "I can't risk losing them again!"

Finally, I see. From his point of view, he can't rejoin his family if he doesn't measure up to them—and even though there's no real basis for this unfounded idea of his, it's clearly what he believes. How can I destroy the legend that's haunting this man? How can I help him get the villagers' approval?

I spend a very long time staring blankly into space, completely lost in my own thoughts. I don't know how long I sit there, but Alfred sits in silence and waits patiently for me to speak, without pressuring me at all.

And finally, a solution starts to form.

I look up into his face. "Trust me," I reassure him. "I'm going to help you."

And just like that, I leave the shed and walk straight back to where I came from: the living room. Once there, I take a look at the clock, which reads 6:26 in the evening. I still have some time left.

I reach for the most recent edition of the newspaper on the pile by the entrance and find the number I'm looking for in the bottom left-hand corner of the front page.

I pick up the receiver and dial it.

Ring ring.

Ring ring.

Ring ri—

"Hello, *Evening Hills* offices. How can I help you?"

After being passed back and forth from one person to another for a while, I eventually end up talking to somebody very helpful who lets me explain my request—a request for something which I hope will help Alfred realize that what *was* is now consigned, once and for all, to the past. As soon as I hang up, the exhaustion I've been accumulating for the whole day begins to make itself felt.

With leaden feet, I drag myself off to my bedroom, set the alarm, and let myself rest under the soft covers.

DAY 18

NEITHER THE pale morning sunlight coming through the window
nor the alarm I set for half past nine
before collapsing into bed last night manages to wake me, and
by the time I've opened my eyes and looked at the clock it's
closer to noon.

Without getting up, I lean over and tug the curtains open.
Outside it's cloudy, but at least it looks calm.

I lie there in bed for a while. Obviously, I was even more
tired than I'd realised.

It's strangely relaxing here, considering that the bed I'm
lounging about in is inside a bedroom which belongs to

two complete strangers who have mysteriously disappeared without leaving a trace, and that in the house my only human contact—I suppose I *can* still say that Alfred is human—is a spirit.

I know that my unwillingness to get up and face the day is at least in part because I know it's going to be a day of waiting for something to happen. Of waiting for the wheels that I set in motion last night to crank out a result.

And of hoping that the result is the one I want.

Eventually, the growling of my tummy gets so loud that I can't put getting up off any longer, though, so I haul myself out of bed and, still wearing the same fluffy pyjamas, walk down the corridor, putting my hair up in a bun as I go.

By the time I'm done, I find myself exactly where I want to be: in the kitchen.

I fill the kettle and put it on the hob, and when it's boiling I make myself some green tea. A quick rummage around in the cupboards reveals a packet of biscuits that I must have missed before, so I put a few on a plate and take them and my steaming mug over to the sofa.

I sit there slowly sipping away and nibbling on the delicious biscuits, listening to the slow, deep ticking of the grandfather clock and staring out of the French windows at the garden.

I could stay here all day.

It's like time doesn't exist.

Like it's not passing at all . . .

. . . until there's the sudden clattering sound of a bicycle being dumped on the pavement outside, and I hear someone banging the gate.

I look up at the clock—it's nearly five!

How can that be? I only just sat down here with my tea . . . but when I pick up the mug, it's stone cold.

With a shrug of impatience and frustration, I jump up, walk over to the front door, and unlock it. When I pull it open, the cold, fresh breeze caresses my cheeks.

I step outside onto the porch and race down the path, searching for the evening newspaper that should have just been delivered.

It's getting really foggy this evening, and my surroundings are so blurry that it's hard to see clearly. I walk barefoot down the path towards the gate and when I get there I'm relieved to find the paper I was waiting for wedged into one of its wrought-iron curlicues.

I pull it out and race back inside, my feet freezing from the icy flagstones, and once I'm indoors again I hold up the front page of the newspaper. There it is, right there: the article I need.

Feeling as though I finally have all the answers, I eat the last biscuit, wash it down with a swig of cold tea, and roll the paper up, tucking it securely under my arm as I head outside.

When I reach the shed I twist the door handle, but it appears to be locked from the inside, so I give a few loud, rapid knocks on the door.

It swings open immediately, and I gratefully bundle myself inside, out of the misty cold.

Before I can show the article to Alfred, however, he speaks.

"Sorry about that—it's a habit of mine. Nobody ever looks in here."

"No worries," I say, my mind on other, more pressing matters.

"Have you got some more questions for me?" he asks gently.

"No," I reply, before adding quickly, as I see his expression grow sad, "I do believe that I might have some good news for you, though."

He waits silently for me to explain myself, and so I unroll the newspaper I've been holding under my arm and pass it over to him. He holds it up in his strong hands, the paper crinkling between his tense fingers. There's confusion on his face, but it's also full of hope, and I study his expression, watching as his eyeballs flit across the words, until a small, lonely tear emerges, falling onto the dusty wooden floor.

When he's done reading, he turns the page to check if there's more, and realizing that that's all there is, he looks up at me and says, "Is this real?"

Suddenly gripped by worry about what his reaction is going to be, I step backwards, unable to reply to his question. Was I a fool to believe that just getting the paper to print an article about him would redeem him from the aftermath of such a life-altering tragedy? Is it possible that just reading the good things people have to say about Alfred Marshall won't have been enough to make him comprehend how much people in the village actually admired him?

The previous night I'd spent about an hour on the phone to a certain Miss Blake—one of the paper's young subeditors—explaining why *The Evening Hills* ought to collect local people's thoughts on Alfred and the Derfla legend. I'd managed to get her attention by explaining my point of view and pointing out a couple of things that hadn't really been given due consideration before.

She'd gone for the idea straightaway. She vaguely remembered the fire, she told me. In her early teens, she and her girlfriends had been *terrified* of the Derfla. Her grandmother had always said that it was awful to do that to somebody—turn him into a monster, even though the police had cleared him of any wrongdoing. Miss Blake hadn't even known that Alfred Marshall had hung himself, but she agreed that it wasn't right that the poor man's reputation should still be tarnished even after his death.

She'd agreed instantly to write an article based on the real facts about the man, and I was certain it would make him realize that by now people had moved on from the silly old legend which was holding him here in the mortal world, and that no one really blamed him for what happened—at least not anymore.

For a moment, neither of us moves.

Then Alfred suddenly launches himself towards me, arms wide open as if to attack me and a crazed look on his face.

Caught off guard, I back away, trying desperately to defend myself by throwing my flailing arms forward . . .

But before I know it, I find myself in the middle of what has to be the most awkward, yet probably the sweetest, hug I've experienced in my whole life.

◎∕◎

I hug Alfred back and we stay like that, unmoving, for a few seconds. His big arms are squeezing me tightly, crushing me without meaning to, almost in a fatherly way—the same way a man would hug his little girl after not having seen her for a long time. I close my eyes, let my body relax, and think about what's coming next.

Crossing over.

I've read plenty over the last few days, all related to spirits, but not a single time have I stumbled across any details about

129

the actual moment of crossing over itself. How does it happen? How can I possibly know if what I've done is enough to release a spirit?

As if Alfred is able to read my thoughts, he backs gently away from me, freeing me from that warm embrace. He brings his index finger to his lips and, gazing at the roof of the shed, he exhales a puff of air from the small gap between his lips, indicating I should keep quiet. I promptly grow attentive, unaware of what it is he might have heard.

His face is turned towards one of the small windows—the one that I stupidly broke during my irresponsible attempt to get inside—so I follow his lead and move closer to the other, which is still intact.

Outside, a blustery wind is shaking the trees and bushes in the garden. The sky has turned very dark, and is filled with churning black clouds which seem intent on swallowing us up.

There's something else too—a harsh cawing noise, distant but rapidly growing in volume.

I peer about worriedly, looking for its source.

And then, in a whirl of shiny black motion which appears to comes out of nowhere, an unkindness of ravens—scores of them—is suddenly spinning in a frantic circle above the shed, turning the already chilling atmosphere even more sinister.

The noise is absolutely deafening, but when I look over at Alfred I see that all his attention is still concentrated on what's happening outside.

One huge raven lands on the sill of the remaining window and, with a violent blow from its shiny beak, smashes the glass, sending me leaping backwards in fear. I run to take shelter behind Alfred—he doesn't flinch, but I can tell that in his head he's debating what to do.

He lets out a gasp and starts to raise his left hand, moving it slowly towards the doorknob.

I grab his arm, feeling my unease grow and becoming increasingly worried about Alfred's intentions.

"Don't go out there," I say, my voice trembling. "We don't know what'll happen."

"Well, we'll never find out if I don't," he answers gently.

I'm still holding tightly onto his arm when he turns to me, his face calm and peaceful for the first time.

"Thank you, Amethyst."

Accompanied by a sinking feeling comes the sudden realisation that this is the last time we two will speak to each other, and I start trying to wish him farewell—but nothing comes out of my mouth. So I just nod and concentrate on trying to keep my composure and hide the fact that my heart is fluttering madly.

He twists the handle, inviting the unwanted inside.

I don't move a single muscle, only watch intently as Alfred steps through the door, ready for whatever his destiny holds in store for him.

The screeching of the ravens intensifies, the sky gets darker still, the wind blows even more wildly, and for one brief, chaotic moment, all of the worst possible outcomes of what's happening start to play out in my mind—all the awful horrors that we might have released . . .

Only to be halted in their tracks by the appearance of an unexpected ray of blindingly bright sunlight.

It cuts through the clouds and strikes Alfred, illuminating his body, sculpting out its every contour.

For a second I can see him properly—I can see the real Alfred: a proud, dignified, handsome man, freed from the weight of guilt and shame that have been crushing him all these years. Even after his death.

At that very same moment, as though by some silent signal, the entire flock of ravens swoops down as one to perch, covering the ground, the tree branches, and the roof of the shed. The chaotic squawking and flapping noises vanish, and the atmosphere instantly grows peaceful.

I watch incredulously as the ray of unearthly light gradually softens my friend's form into nothingness.

An instant before his body fades completely away he manages to turn around and look me straight in the eyes, and he smiles. I take a mental picture of his happy face, happier than I've ever seen it before, looking for the first time at peace—as though the weight of the problems that had been keeping him bound to the earth was now dissolving, allowing him to fly away and return to his beloved family.

In what feels like both an eternal yet ephemeral moment of time, I feel as though I'm as light as the air itself.

Then, as one, the ravens take to the sky in a blizzard of wings, beaks, and claws, and the entire flock of them flaps silently off over the trees towards the hills.

I look at the lawn around me, strewn with inky-black raven feathers.

It truly is the quiet after the storm.

DAY 19

A T LUNCHTIME, I eventually roll out of bed. It's been a quiet, peaceful night—both as regards the weather and my mind. Right after Alfred crossed over, I seemed to just let go of everything, immersed in the happiness of the moment.

Carefully avoiding looking in the mirror, I take a hot, steamy shower before picking up my not-so-clean clothes from the floor, combing my hair back, and heading in the direction of the kitchen.

I walk calmly along the corridor, enjoying the sense of loneliness that comes from knowing that now it's all just about me. No more ghosts creating confusion. No more creepy nightmares. *Just me.*

I reach for the same bowl I ate from during my first few days in the house, fill it with some milk—which I notice is coming up to its best-before date—then grab the last few cookies from the jar on the shelf and finish them off as well, filling up my empty stomach nicely.

But as I walk in front of the fridge to throw the milk carton into the rubbish and put the bowl in the sink, I notice something shocking that I would swear wasn't there ten minutes ago.

The *Who are you?* that I left on the fridge door a few days before—it's changed.

It now reads, *Who are you, Amethyst?*

Unable to believe my eyes, I freeze in shock and the glass bowl slides from my limp fingers, smashing into smithereens when it hits the ground.

There's somebody here.

I can sense it.

I'm still not alone, after all.

I spin around, in search of some clue that might help me understand what I'm getting myself into this time, but everything is as peaceful and still as usual. I feel light-headed, so I throw myself down on the couch for a few minutes while I gather my thoughts.

Whoever left that message is in here with me—in the house. It must be somebody that knows me well enough to write my name, but then why ask who I am?

Confused by the question, I stand up, walk back over to the fridge, and, in the blink of an eye, slide away the letters that were creating my confusion into a jumble by the handle, leaving only *Amethyst.*

After changing the sentence, I stand there for a moment studying the room around me. I feel certain that I'm not alone—that there's a presence there with me. But I can't see who it is. And whatever it is, it's not alive.

Or at least, that's what I suppose.

I pull out a chair from under the dining table, move it over to the bookshelf, and climb up onto it to get *Spiritual Relief* again. It takes me a moment to find it, and when I do, it occurs to me that it's not exactly where I'd left it. Never mind. I get down off the chair and open the book as quickly as I can. Remembering that I'd skipped the chapter "Talk to the Spirit," I flick through the pages with my thumb until I find it.

This section contains a description of the various ways to communicate with a spirit, a common one being through a Ouija board—also known as a "talking board"—which is supposed to act as a point of connection between the world of the living and the world of the dead. The book has a part which provides a detailed explanation of how to make your own: all you need is a flat surface bearing the letters of the alphabet, the numbers from 0 to 9, and the words "yes," "no," and "goodbye." It says that an effective substitute for the planchette, the heart-shaped little pointer with wheels on the bottom which you're supposed to use to let the spirits talk, can be a small glass placed upside-down on the surface, so I take one from a cupboard in the kitchen and get to work on making my own Ouija board.

Remembering the old Bakelite telephone on the console table by the front door, I make a leap of imagination and pull open the little drawer in the table—and in fact, inside there are a pen and some large sheets of plain paper, which I grab.

Following Ms. Bisset's instructions to the letter, I write down everything she says is needed and place it all on the kitchen table, with the upturned glass in the middle.

When I'm all set, I put my right index finger on top of the glass and ask out loud:

"Is there anybody here?"

I wait, but there's no sign of anything.

"Is there anybody here?" I repeat, this time sounding less afraid.

Feeling a slow dragging movement under my finger, I close my eyes for a second to try to hold my fear in, and then open them again to look at where the glass has ended up.

"Yes."

At this point, I decide to come out with my main question right away. No more beating around the bush.

"Who are you?" I ask.

It takes about three seconds before the glass starts to move again, and as I watch, it changes position over the letters, first sliding across to Y, then to O.

And then to U.

And that's when I let it go. I take my finger away from it as soon as I have put the letters together.

It spells the word "you."

Suddenly extremely frightened, I leave everything where it is, forgetting all about Vivien Bisset's warning to always end a session properly, and, despite knowing that no wall or lock would present an obstacle to a spirit, I run down the hall to my room.

As soon as I'm inside, I realize how dark it's already grown, and for some unknown reason I find myself opening the wardrobe door, climbing in, and closing myself inside as though it were the most natural thing in the world to be hiding in a cramped little space that smells of mothballs and lavender.

I try to keep as quiet as I can. Covering my mouth with one hand, I breathe slowly through my nose while the scene that I just experienced keeps replaying itself over and over in my head.

Feeling totally impotent and jumping in terror at each of the little noises that come from every corner of the house, I sit there in that dark space for a long time before eventually falling asleep.

☙❧

"Through the wind and through the clouds, we will rise up from the ground. Over hills, above the trees, we will ride the breeze like bumblebees."

I open my eyes and hear this strange ditty coming from somewhere within my room.

I push one of the wardrobe doors open slightly and peek cautiously though the narrow crack. Sitting there on the bed is a girl with long black hair, her back turned to me.

"Hand in hand, exploring the seven seas," she sings, "you and I will forever be at our ease."

Despite my efforts, the wardrobe door makes a loud creak as I push it open, but the girl, who seems somehow to be already aware of my presence, doesn't turn around and says, "You're safe. You can come out now."

My eyes widen, as if she knows my secret—a secret that I still have to discover myself.

I open the doors to reveal myself, taking a better look as I do so at Akiko, who appears more serene than ever before, as if suddenly our roles had been reversed, turning me into the fearful little girl that she was the first time I met her.

"Did you know I was in here?" I ask.

She ignores the question and begins to sing her song again from the beginning.

"Why are you here?" I break in.

"I could ask you the same thing," she answers, her eyes staring into mine. "This is *my* room."

I don't reply but simply walk over and sit down next to her on the bed. She has pale green almond-shaped eyes, and her dark hair is straight but thick, framing an innocent-looking face. In her hands she's holding a wooden heart, and when I look up at the white wall in front of me I see that the heart-shaped painting which made such a nice contrast is no longer there, suggesting that the object in Akiko's hands is indeed the one that used to hang in that empty space.

"Did you make that?" I wonder aloud.

"*We* made it," she says, moving her eyes from the object to me.

I feel my cheeks going red, unsure as to why but feeling a sense of embarrassment, as though I should remember about doing something *with* her, until she quickly adds, "Avery and I—don't you see?" She turns the wooden heart over, pointing at the letters painted on it.

I feel relieved to know that I am not part of all this, but at the same time I want to know more. Avery said that Akiko died not too long ago. Is she a ghost? Is she stuck here because of her connection with Avery? Maybe she doesn't want to leave him on his own?

I stretch out a hand and ask, "Could I take a look at it? It's very pretty."

Akiko tightens her grip on the frame, as though it's too important for anybody else to hold, but then relents and hands it over to me.

I study the front once more, feeling the thick paint under my fingers. When I turn it over, I see the word "forever" written in marker pen in the same handwriting as the letters on the front. I must spend a moment too long examining it, because Akiko reaches over and snatches it out of my hands, slipping it into the safe little pocket on the front of her collared dress.

"So are you and this Avery close friends?" I ask, pretending not to know who she's talking about.

"Of course!" she answers defensively.

"Where did you meet?" I ask, despite already knowing the answer.

"He lives right there," answers the little girl, pointing towards the wall behind my back.

"So *when* did you meet?"

She thinks for a moment before finally coming out with an answer.

"When I moved here—he was the only friend I had."

"Don't you have many friends?"

She shakes her head, adding, "I only need one." And then her face grows sad.

"The other kids are mean to me because I look different," she continues, "but he's different too, so we understand each other."

"What's different about him?" I ask, curious to know.

"Everything," she says, staring at me as if that was the silliest question I could have asked. "He doesn't ask for anything, but he gives you everything."

As I hear those words coming out of her mouth, I find myself completely agreeing with her. But at the same time I realize that it's a bit of a surreal kind of conversation to be having with a girl this little—one who can't be more than twelve years old at the most. She does seem much more mature than her age, especially in the way she expresses herself, but, at the same time, her youth shines through in the way she behaves.

I gaze at her long, pretty, silky hair flowing over the blanket as she stands up to gracefully place the heart back in the spot where it belongs.

"Do you like this boy, then?" I ask, feeling almost like a big sister.

"He's *very* special to me!" she exclaims, then brings her hands up to her face to hide the blush that instantly darkens her peachy cheeks. As soon as she has managed to conceal her emotions, she adds, "But we're just good friends."

Tickled by the childlike intensity of her reaction, I nod, hiding an amused smile.

"He deserves someone to care about him. And I do," she says, immediately covering her mouth, as if that last part wasn't supposed to have slipped out.

"What about his family?" I ask, surprised by her words.

In her eyes I can see the same sadness that I saw before on Avery's. She looks away, trying to hide it, but then says, "His parents don't care the way I do."

"How do you know that?"

"I just do!" she snaps.

I wake up from my dream in complete darkness, realizing that I'm still inside the wardrobe.

Alone.

DAY 20

I OPEN THE wardrobe door and glance over at the clock on the bedside table: 11:40 a.m. I have to remember to set the alarm or else I'm going to mess my sense of time up for good. Though it might already be a bit late for that, to be honest.

Stiff all over, I climb out of the cramped space my body has moulded itself to during the night, stretching as I walk down the hall to the main part of the house for some late breakfast. Or some early lunch.

I open the French country kitchen cabinet, reaching up as high as I can for the oatmeal that I noticed up there not too long ago. I cook it on the hob in a small pot, and as I do

I let my imagination wander, trying to imagine where Alfred is right now, if he can see me from wherever that might be, if he's finally happy, if he found his family. I can have no sure answer to any of these questions, but I somehow *know* that he is at peace.

I can't even imagine how awful it must have been for him to be stuck here, in a world full of hate towards him. Hate which was undeserved, to say the least, and all because of a silly made-up story that no one even cared about anymore. Five long years with no one knowing what he was going through and no one to talk to and nobody to share his feelings with. Until I came into his life—or, I should probably say, his death. But why me? Why would I be able to see him? How did *I*—a perfect stranger—manage to help him so easily?

The focus of my thoughts suddenly switches to Avery and our last conversation, right before the fight. The fact that he was so mysterious about this whole situation suggests to me that he's hiding something. He knows something I don't—maybe something he doesn't want me to know about. But then why does he act the way he does when he's *with* me? Why open up to me, and be so . . . so *there*, if he's not really willing to help me? Could it be that he thought it was dangerous to mess about with the fragile threads between the two dimensions? Is there any chance that both Avery *and* the Blooms had always been aware of the gardener's presence— but were just too afraid to help him leave?

All of these hypotheses start appearing in my thoughts as though I've already made my mind up about what's happening, but at the same time, there are so many other things that still need an explanation. To start with an easy one, where are Amabel and Marvin? Did they *deliberately* leave me here alone? I can't believe they would do that; it wouldn't make any sense. And what is the story behind Akiko? Why does she keep appearing to me in my dreams? Is that even what they *are*? They certainly feel deeper and more real than dreams—almost as if they were visions or something.

When I've finished eating, I clean up and put everything back where it belongs, then go over to the entrance hall and squint through the peephole, unable to shake the feeling that somebody is watching me all the time. But there's nobody there—as I expected. I grab my shoes—a pair of worn-out white All Stars I've used so much that they look far older than they actually are—and as I put them on I remember how much I used to like going for walks. Long ones. I didn't have to be with anyone else; being on my own was never a problem for me.

And then one specific memory comes back to me.

I am strolling up a hill. It's quite steep, and I'm alone. Once I reach the top, the breathtaking view of White Hills spread out below me makes me feel more alive than ever before. I vividly remember the mosaic of fields, with just a few cottages dotted here and there, and the contrast they make with the jumble of pretty old buildings clustered together around the little square at the centre of the village.

The fog is blurring the colours of the twilight, blending the rich blues and the pale pinks wonderfully, and a few houses already have their lights on while others have got a fire burning, as the smoke emerging from their chimneys shows. But hardly anybody ever actually spends any time up here, and all the rest of them miss out on seeing this amazing view.

Snapping out of my daydream, I come back to my senses,

realising that my body must have somehow made its way to the front gate by itself.

Stepping forward and ready to leave the house for the first time in weeks, I suddenly hear a ripping noise under one of my feet. I peer down at the source of the sound, bewildered to find that there appears to be a note stuck under the sole. I lift my foot so that I can collect the two pieces I've accidentally torn apart and crouch down on the path.

Placing them together on the ground next to each other, I read:

Under the ground, beneath the house,
you will scamper like a mouse.
We will cheer, that I can bet,
to a night you'll never forget.

A few blank lines, and then:

21st of October. 9:00 p.m.
Our secret place.

I read the note over and over again, the weird little rhyme making me feel increasingly uncomfortable. Then, on an impulse, I turn the note over—and instantly regret that I have. In the centre, my name has been written with the same black pen as the rest of the message.

I try to get my head around this sinister clue, wondering first of all how it got here in the first place, and secondly who would have left such a mysterious thing for me—and then I remember something.

The song Akiko was singing, sitting on her bed last night.

This is the same kind of poem, except that the words are different. Could she be behind this? What does this note mean?

I analyse each word, starting at the beginning. The first line seems to hint that there's something underneath this house—what she calls "our secret place." If it weren't for my name written on the back of the piece of paper, I would presume that it was meant for somebody else, but it's obviously no coincidence. Our secret place . . . where would that be? The place I've seen Akiko most is in the bedroom, if I'm not mistaken—maybe there's something in there?

I move on to the second line, trying to understand why we would be cheering, and the only thing that I can possibly think of is that it might be Akiko's birthday.

I struggle to remember if there were any specific dates in the family album that I found in the Blooms' bedroom, but I just can't remember, no matter how hard I try.

All of a sudden I realise that I must have zoned out for a while, as the soft light of the sun has now grown so dim that it's left me in almost complete darkness again. I feel the coldness in the air, freezing the tip of my nose. Picking up the two halves of the note from the path, I grasp them in my hand while I walk inside, back into that warm yet desolate home.

Without wasting any time, I go directly to the master bedroom, still illuminated by the last faint light of evening coming through the French doors. I rush over to the bed, checking underneath to find the box still where I left it. I remove the lid and take out the album, opening it at the second page, at the very same picture of Akiko blowing on those colourful little candles. I check for any clues, but the only number I can see is the date, 1996, on the first page, right under the title. Nothing else.

Aware of the fact that there's something more pressing that I need to take care of right now, I carefully put the album back in place, just like the last time I was in here.

I look around, and my eye is drawn to the trapdoor in the ceiling which leads to the attic. It would be so easy to climb up there and get the answers I need, but at the same time, a voice in my head keeps telling me to look for the "secret place" instead, as though that might reveal what this mystery is all about.

Feeling as though someone's eyes are on me all the time and unable to help myself from constantly peering about me, I tiptoe out of the bedroom.

When I get back to my bedroom, the words "beneath" and "secret" keep going round in my head. I immediately check under the bed, but there's absolutely nothing—not even dust.

I start taking a better look at the desk in search of clues, and accidentally knock a glass full of marbles and pencils to the floor. The small glass spheres mostly settle in the same spot at the centre of the worn rug, so I get down on my knees to collect them all, feeling as though this might be the sign I was waiting for. I slide the rug away, hoping to discover something that might remotely resemble an opening to an underground floor, but there's nothing there at all—the wooden floor is perfectly solid and there's absolutely nothing peculiar about it.

I slump dejectedly down to the floor with my back against the wall. And that's when I see it: one single marble, over there by the wardrobe, far away from all the others.

I crawl over to that side of the room and pick it up. I stare at it for a second, thinking about what you'd be able to hide under a wardrobe this gigantic.

Climbing to my feet, I squeeze myself into the gap between the side of the huge piece of furniture and the wall and push with all my might, using my body as a lever.

After I've given it a couple of shoves and am starting to feel my strength failing, I stop, and with delight find that I've managed to move it enough to reveal a semicircular trapdoor with an iron handle attached to the edge in the floor.

Despite my excitement about my discovery, though, I'm absolutely exhausted—my forehead is burning and my face is dripping with sweat.

Deciding to be cautious, I lie down to rest for a minute, but, overwhelmed by fatigue and wrapped in the warm embrace of the soft blanket, I can't stop myself from falling into a deep, deep sleep.

DAY 21

THE NEXT morning, I wake up earlier than usual.

Yesterday evening, I didn't manage to take a proper look at that opening in the floor, still half covered by the massive wardrobe—but in the light of day I'm almost thankful that I didn't decide to go down there at night.

I slip a hand inside the front pocket of my jeans, where I put the sinister note for safekeeping. Its choice of words makes it sound so much *creepier* that it needs to be. If someone wants to meet me, why be so mysterious about it?

Whoever left this for me obviously already knew where to find me. Could it be another ghost? Could it be the same person who wrote to me using the magnetic letters on the fridge?

At the thought of this last possibility, a shiver runs down my back.

I stand up and, after giving myself a quick once-over in the mirror, head towards the kitchen.

My name is still there, crookedly spelled out across the shiny door of the fridge, and I'm reminded once again of the weird feeling I get every time I try to loosen up and lower my guard.

I grasp the handle and pull it open. There's not much left inside, but my eyes immediately alight upon something that wasn't there the last time I looked: a fluffy cupcake with just one pink candle in the middle, right at the centre of the rack.

A word comes to mind—"celebrate."

Is this some kind of game? Because I'm not finding it amusing.

I grab the tiny cake and place it on top of the dining table. There's a good chance that the same person who left me the note also put this cupcake in the fridge for me to see, so I scrutinise it carefully. I no longer even bother looking around the room to see if anybody's there—the fear that's been dogging me for the last few days is finally turning into anger, and I'm feeling increasingly eager to find out who's behind all of this.

In the hope of finding some kind of clue inside it, I start poking away at the cake until I've reduced it to nothing more than a pile of crumbs—but crumbs are all that remain.

Instantly overcome with guilt, I clean up the mess I've made and collect the shards of the broken bowl from where I left them on the floor the other day.

In desperate need of some energy, I prepare my usual breakfast, and when I'm done eating I head towards the other part of the house, tempted for a second to enter the Blooms' bedroom but then opting for the bathroom instead.

I turn on the hot water in the shower and wait a few minutes until the air is thick with warm steam, then take off my clothes and climb right into the stream.

I try as hard as I can to forget about everything—to disconnect and just enjoy the pleasure of relaxing for a while. But something's stopping me.

Why am I still here?

That's the question I keep asking. If the excuse I'd been giving myself—and everybody else—for being here was working for the first few days, after all that's happened I'm not sure it's still valid. Is it really wise to stay in this wonderful yet strangely creepy house when the Blooms seem not to care enough about me to come back, and the house itself seems to want me out of here?

What if, maybe, there's something more?

That's what I probably keep telling myself—that there's something to *know*, something it's up to me to figure out.

There's a sudden flash of lightning, bright enough to penetrate my closed eyelids. I blink them open and see another flash through the little window behind me, followed by a rumble of thunder. Bad weather on the way.

Placing my right foot on the rim of the bathtub, I reach up with both hands to grab the pole that holds the shower curtain and hoist myself upwards to face the window, which would otherwise be too high for me to see through.

I stare out at the backyard, almost missing Alfred's presence. Although it scared me at the beginning, it actually managed to make me feel *safer* and *less* lonely once I knew about his situation.

But now I'm alone, and all I can do is gaze over at Avery's unlit window wondering if he's home and what he might be doing.

My eyes begin to wander from the window to the rest of the house around it. So well does the building match the forbidding colour of the approaching dark clouds that it's almost invisible against them, giving it an unnervingly spectral appearance.

Tired of balancing there on the edge of the tub, I step down, wrap a big, white bath towel around myself, grab my clothes, and make my way to the opposite side of the house— my bedroom.

❧

I reach backwards and push the door shut behind me, too incredulous at what I find there in front of me to even bother turning round while I do it: a dress that I've never seen before is hanging from one of the flower-shaped knobs of the old wooden wardrobe.

Keeping my distance, as though it might be alive and ready to attack, I examine it thoroughly.

It's a wonderful midi dress in pale yellow, with a straight hem and scalloped three-quarters sleeves. A matching white scalloped collar decorates the neckline ever so gently, while a row of small white buttons runs down to the part where the skirt starts to flare out at the waist. On the right side of the bodice there's a small pocket, from which the corner of a note protrudes.

Still standing by the door with my hand gripping the handle, I feel unsure about what I should do next: leave the room, or shut myself inside?

Deciding on the spur of the moment to ignore my fears, I pick a third option and walk slowly over towards the dress, luxuriating in its old-fashioned beauty.

I stretch out my right hand in order to take the note hidden by the fabric of the pocket, and as I do, a loud crash of thunder makes me jump so violently that I bring my other hand to my heart to check that it's still beating and to try to calm myself down.

When my heartbeat returns to normal—or at least close enough—I open my right hand and read the crumpled note.

Amethyst.

That's all it says.

I look back at the dress, feeling more confused than ever, and totally unable to comprehend why someone would play games like this with me.

I sit on the bed and look at the clock, which tells me that it's seven thirty in the evening, before focusing my bleary eyes on the floor under the wardrobe, studying the stained half moon which is peeking through, partially hidden by the hulking piece of antique furniture.

It takes me a while to make my mind up, but in the end I decide to play along. I get to my feet and change into the dress—which, to my surprise, fits me perfectly—then sit by the desk and open one of the drawers, finding a nude-look lip balm which I apply to my dry lips, making them instantly look about a hundred times nicer. I then attempt an updo for my hair, leaving the sides of my bangs out to frame my face and soften my strong features before putting the rest into a messy bun which I secure to my head with a handful of bobby pins I find in a tub in one of the drawers.

The last thing left to do is to free up the trapdoor in the floor. I use the same technique as the previous day—wedging myself between the wardrobe and the wall and pushing with my whole body. After a few minutes of struggling, I finally manage to get it out of the way.

I then pop quickly to the kitchen, where the clock reads 8:45 p.m., telling me that I've only got fifteen minutes left to get down there—to "our secret place"—and bring a conclusion to this elaborate plan.

I pick up the flashlight that I found in the Blooms' bedroom from where I left it by the sink, but when I switch it on it starts flickering and its beam grows dimmer and dimmer until it's just a vague glow. I unscrew the back and see with irritation that the batteries inside are caked with rust.

A quick rummage through the kitchen drawers looking for spares is no help, so I open the drawer that contains all the candles and matches and light one, sheltering the flame carefully with a cupped hand while I walk back to the room where I started.

As ready to go now as I suppose I ever will be, I place the candle on the floor next to the old trapdoor, grab hold of the handle with both hands, and heave up on it with all my strength. The thought that it might be locked crosses my mind for an instant, but I don't give up and keep tugging until, to my relief, I feel something give, and it swings upwards.

I pick up the candle that will light my way and start walking down the narrow, irregular stairs which are revealed beneath the trapdoor, and which take me deeper and deeper under the ground.

The farther down I get, the less light from the bedroom reaches me. After a few minutes the stairs stop, and I finally reach a flat place. Before me in the flickering candlelight I see a narrow corridor stretching off into the darkness.

There's no light apart from that of my candle. No sound other than my footsteps.

I set off walking, accompanied by a growing sensation of fear for my life, wondering as I go why in the world I've decided to do something this dangerous. I try to convince myself that it's the right thing to do, that I *need* to do this in order to give a face to the person who has been watching me all this time.

I follow the tunnel. There are no side passages branching off, so I'm confident that I'm going in the right direction, and as I walk I observe the few details that the weak light of the candle permits me to see: the tunnel appears to be cave-like, hewn directly out of raw, damp stone. Its surface is uneven, and there are patches of mould growing here and there.

The strange burrow seems never to come to an end, so I decide to speed up my pace a little and focus my energies on getting to wherever it is I'm supposed to be, bracing myself for whatever I might be about to encounter.

Suddenly, the tunnel curves to the right and I see a faint glow coming from as far in the distance as my eye can make out. I start walking even faster, anxious now to know. Dozens of thoughts are buzzing about in my head but I push them all away, positive that once I reach the light—which is now growing stronger and stronger by the second—I'll have the answer to everything.

And then there I am. Halfway along what feels like the longest tunnel in the world, it widens out into a small circular chamber where three tunnels meet, which I'm now standing in the middle of. I look back down the tunnel I've arrived from, and study the other two opening off at my sides. Unsure of what to do, I stand there, motionless.

The dark walls are lit by the countless flickering candles that somebody has placed on the ground, which create a dusky atmosphere. Between them are a blanket and some cushions.

My own small candle still in hand, I step onto the blanket in my white All Stars and gaze up at the ceiling, from which a heavy iron cross hangs, instantly bringing a sinister thought to mind.

Sacrifice.

Is *that* what this is all about?

A powerful desire to get out of there takes hold of me, urging me to escape from this dangerous, frightening place, but it's too late—there are footsteps behind me.

I spin round so fast that my candle goes flying out of my hand and rolls away on the stone floor.

"Hey."

As he speaks, Avery looks at me with a smile on his face. He's carrying a basket, the same one I saw the day we shared our picnic. His hair is neatly brushed to one side, and he's looking his best in a simple blue shirt and black jeans.

Has *he* done all this? Is he the one who's been spying on me? Playing games?

Scaring me to death?

"What are you doing here?" I ask, upset at the thought.

Avery looks at me as if I'm making a fool of myself.

"I wanted to see you."

"Why would you do all this? Why not just *ask* to see me?" I say, my voice rising.

"That's not my style," he jokes, and Akiko's words about him instantly come to mind.

"So what are we doing here?"

"We're going to have a nice dinner together."

I fold my arms over my chest.

"I don't have any food, and I'm not planning to go back to get any," I say, still sceptical about his motives.

He points at the basket he's just placed on the blanket.

"Good job I spent all day cooking, then," he says.

I stare at him, challenging him to look me in the face, and, without breaking eye contact, he does. What I've gone through has been a real nightmare to me, but the smile on his face seems to say that it's all just a silly game to him, and it's driving me insane.

"Why are you doing this?" I ask once more.

"I've already told you," he says, moving some cushions out of the way.

"Why did you have to be so mysterious about it?"

"I just wanted to surprise you. Now can you *please* sit down with me?" He reaches for my hand and gently drags me down next to him.

I feel my cheeks redden, but hold my emotions at arm's length.

"You scared me. You have no idea how much."

Avery looks at me, confusion and concern in his face. He pauses a moment before speaking, then says simply, "I'm sorry. I really didn't mean to upset you."

His words sound so sincere that I can't help believing him,

so with a baffled, resigned sigh I make myself comfortable on one of the many cushions dotted around.

He starts to unpack the food he's prepared for us and serve it on paper plates, and I pour some water into a cup. While I study his movements, I suddenly remember that the last time we saw each other things didn't go awfully well, and that I really ought to apologize to him, so I whisper, "I'm sorry."

He's so busy finding room on the blanket for all the food he's cooked that he doesn't raise his eyes but just shakes his head slightly and says, "Don't worry about it."

Even though he isn't looking at me, I can hear the pain in his words, and a fresh wave of guilt at having laid into him the way I did washes over me. But I mustn't let all that stop us from having a nice time, so I let it go.

We start eating the portions of mushroom risotto that he has carefully packed into mugs, and as I savour the taste of my first mouthful I can't stop myself from asking, "Where did you learn to cook so well?"

He swallows.

"Growing up I had to learn by myself. Eventually."

Yet again, Akiko's words come to mind, and so I risk another question.

"Are you close to your parents?"

Avery takes his time answering, and I wonder if it might have been inappropriate to ask, but after a while he replies.

"I used to be." He lets out a tense breath. "But over time my family fell apart."

"I'm sorry, I didn't mean to—" I say, but he stops me with a smile.

"Don't apologize. It's fine." He takes another forkful of the risotto and continues. "Dad had always had problems with alcohol, ever since I was little. He could get violent at times. When I was eighteen, it just got so bad that I couldn't stand it anymore."

The sadness evident in his words is starting to make me feel guilty for having asked him about his past.

"But I couldn't leave the house, because I didn't want to leave my mum alone with him . . . among other things."

I nod as he recounts these personal details.

"A few years ago, when I was twenty," he goes on, "there was this huge fight in the house. I came home from university for the weekend and found my dad beating up my mum. Again. I walked into the room and I stood up to him. And after that, he never bothered us again."

"Do you know where he is?" I ask.

"No—and honestly, I couldn't care less. I'm just glad he's leaving my mum alone," he says, and he sounds completely honest.

Noticing that instead of eating my food, I'm just sitting there looking miserable, Avery attempts to bring a smile back to my face.

"You look lovely, by the way."

"Thank you!" I exclaim, taking the collar of my dress between my fingers. I fake a silly smile, aware of the fact that it might well have been him who bought this pretty outfit for me.

Feeling the momentary tension between us fade, I start enjoying my food again. One after another, I try each of the dishes Avery has brought, expressing my amazement at his skill in the kitchen with a series of delighted *Oooooh!*s, and we chat away happily all through the night.

Considering that we're in something that's pretty much a cave, it's surprisingly warm and cosy down here.

I love it. I'm having a wonderful time.

After a few hours of eating and laughing, I collapse against the wall. Avery joins me, sitting right next to me in the same position. Neither of us says a word; we both focus on the silence around us. Such a peaceful atmosphere—and in the creepiest place I've ever visited in my entire life. Almost unbelievable.

Unexpectedly, I feel Avery's hand gently brushing my cheek before ending up behind my head. His lips are suddenly on mine, and I close my eyes and let all of my pent-up emotions pour out into what must be the best kiss I've ever given; soft, but overflowing with passion.

And when the kiss comes to an end, it takes me a while before I'm ready to let it go. I keep my eyes closed and feel Avery's cheek against mine, hear his voice whispering into my ear.

"Happy birthday, Amethyst."

DAY 22

WHAT?

I open my eyes and look around, perplexed: there's nobody here—just me.

How is that possible? Where's Avery? Was it all a dream? No—no, it wasn't!

Everything I felt was real. All of these candles around me, the food, the cushions. Everything here is real.

So where's Avery?

Wondering why on earth he would leave me there like that, I get to my feet and stand at the centre of the chamber looking around me, anxiously waiting for him to come back.

I stand there for a long time.

But he's gone.

When I realize that there's absolutely no point in waiting any longer, I pick up one candle, blow out the others, and make my way back to the start of the tunnel which will take me to my bedroom.

Eventually I get to the stairs and start climbing, thinking gratefully that in a few minutes I should finally see the light again. When I do, and am finally back in the world above ground, I make sure to close the trapdoor over the hole. But I don't bother pushing the wardrobe over it.

I take off my yellow dress, hang it carefully inside the wardrobe, climb into my pyjamas, and start getting ready to go to bed.

It's 1:10 in the morning—time to get some sleep.

◎◎

The sound of raindrops drumming on the window awakens me, yet makes me feel sleepy at the same time. I'm enjoying the warmth of the cosy blanket wrapped around me, which seems to be telling me to stay in bed and never get up. But the alarm clock is shouting that it's already 10:45.

With my strength replenished and last night's tiredness only a memory, I sit up in bed, look out the window at the blustery rainstorm which is thoroughly soaking the garden, and take a moment to think the situation through.

Right away I come up against a few things that still don't quite make sense.

1) Avery organised a nice dinner for us, but I can't really believe that it's him who's been playing these games with me;

2) When I read the note again, I notice with puzzlement that he called the tunnel "our secret place"—what does he mean by that?

3) Why would he think that it was my birthday? And most importantly, why go to such lengths to spend some time with me, only then to just vanish like that?

Even more confused than before, I eventually climb out of bed and, following what is by now my daily routine, I walk down the hall to the main part of the house for some late breakfast. There's no milk left, so I drink a glass of water and toast some stale bread. As I'm spreading it with salted butter, I hear a thud coming from the living room.

I turn around: a book has fallen from the bookcase to the floor.

I walk over and pick it up—it's *Spiritual Relief*. Is this some spirit's way of communicating with me? Is there something in here I need to read?

I carry the book to the table, lay it open there, and wait for something to happen. But, predictably, nothing does.

I'm certain about the fact that someone is here, in the house. In fact, I'm 100 percent positive of it, and that might be the reason I can't leave this place just yet.

All of a sudden, a thought crosses my mind—one so awful it takes my breath away.

I sit there, the book in front of me, mentally reviewing everything that has happened since I came to this house and focusing on the very beginning: the day I met the Blooms.

What if something bad has happened to Amabel and Marvin? What if they need my help? What if they were never alive to begin with?

My hands gripping the book, I take a deep breath, unsure of what my next move should be. I walk over to the bookshelf, ready to put the book back in place, but then another title on the shelf seizes my attention.

The Reverend Mansion.

I pick it up, not sure what to expect.

Opening the first page, I see the title again, followed by the name of the author, Nicholas Goodman, right above the date—1975.

On the following page is a picture of a house with a similar structure to that of the Blooms', but a bit bigger and more cosmopolitan looking—the picture is dated 1923.

And as I leaf through the pages, I see more pictures of the same house over the years, from when it first changed hands and became the property of the first reverend of White Hills, Mr. Smith, through its first renovation about fifty years later, right up to photos in which it looks almost exactly as it does now that it belongs to Mr. and Mrs. Bloom.

There's a chapter called "The Underground Path" which explains the reason for the tunnel under the house. As I start reading, I wonder to myself how I could possibly not have thought to ask Avery about it after spending so much time down there with him the previous night. Never mind—I'm too anxious to discover the answer to waste any more time wondering about last night, so I dedicate my attention to the words before me.

Apparently, the tunnel was dug at the same time the house was built at the request of its original owner. He seemingly had a slightly obsessive desire to be connected at all times with his beloved church, even when the weather—or some other mysterious, unspecified impediment—made it impossible to reach.

By the time Mr. Smith had managed to create a nice little community in White Hills, he'd become an influential, important man. And as he got richer and richer, there came a point where he decided to give something back to his village by opening right behind his delightful abode a hospital, the Smith Medical Centre, which was eventually converted into a private mansion—the same private mansion which is now Avery's family home.

Once building work on the hospital was completed, Mr. Smith decided to dig further tunnels connecting all three of the places which were most important to him, uniting them underneath the ground via a single, dark passageway.

After Mr. Smith's death, a new owner moved into his property—Mr. Goodman, the author of this book and the next reverend of the village.

Mr. Goodman explains that as he was unable to afford to maintain the land the hospital was built on, he had to let it go up for sale. That was when Avery's father bought it and decided to close up the passage under the ground.

The book ends with a section full of detailed before-and-after shots of the house, the hospital, and the church.

I put the book back where I found it and gaze out through the big French windows. The rain is still pouring down, and the bitter chill of the autumn weather is palpable, but the heat of the kiss that Avery and I shared keeps me warm inside.

I find myself staring at his window, my head bursting with questions about him.

About us.

But even though I'm tempted to flick my lights on and off so that we can meet, I don't—I want to save that meeting, hold on to it so that I've got an excuse to see him again.

And I wait, hoping for him to make a move.

Not long after, it suddenly occurs to me that my mind has completely switched off. And that I'm sick and tired of always fighting to know more. So I sit there on that stiff couch and just wait for something to happen, hardly even moving.

I let the day and the night go by, gazing passively out of the window at the rain falling onto the grass.

DAY 23

THROUGH THE blanket covering my face, I hear a creaking noise, as though a door in the house were being opened.

I pull the blanket away from one half-opened eye to peek out at my surroundings, and immediately notice that I appear to be in my bedroom, and yet that it's somehow not quite the *same* bedroom. I sit myself up and take a good look around me.

The white walls that I liked so much are now covered in wallpaper, its floral pattern covering everything and leaving no plain space on the walls. I gaze at the desk, no longer pale white but instead a bright, cherrywood tint, matching the rest of the furniture. Even the sheets feel different.

My heart racing, I climb out of bed. Where am I?

I turn around and reach for the doorknob—I give it a twist, and the door opens onto the same corridor I've walked down so many times before. But again, it doesn't look like it normally does: the walls are darker, almost as if they've aged all of a sudden.

In the darkness, I force my uncooperative feet to move towards the living room, the room closest to my bedroom, all the while feeling certain that somebody is watching me.

As I tiptoe down the hall I try my best to keep calm until I eventually reach my destination—except that it now looks nothing like the living room I was expecting. The layout, with its open-plan kitchen, is still the same, but nothing else is the way I remember it. From the kitchen—so modern and boring compared to the French country style of before—to the big old couch that looks completely different to the stiff but adorable sofa I've spent so much time happily curled up on.

Everything is different.

I stand in front of the couch and hold my left hand out, reaching for it.

But when my fingers make contact with the fabric, I shiver—and to my surprise, it's suddenly daytime.

And everything is back to normal.

Was I *sleepwalking*? Have I done it before?

The house looks as wonderful as ever. It must have been a dream.

I take a seat, and, unbidden, my eyes go to the book, *The Reverend Mansion*, which I was reading the previous day, as though suggesting that my subconscious must have projected all those images into my mind while I was sleeping.

Then, just when I'm starting to feel like I'm making sense of the situation, telling myself that I'm not crazy after all and that there's always an explanation for everything, I hear the sound of a door closing.

Unable to tell exactly which one it was, I stand up and run towards where the sound came from—the hall to the left, where the bathroom, the master bedroom, and the basement are.

I get to the end of the corridor to find all three doors are shut. It's obvious that there's not a moment to waste, so I follow my intuition and go for the door on the left—the basement. Which this time is unlocked.

I throw it open—and see two shadows standing there side by side, right in front of me, only to then disappear in the blink of an eye.

Leaving me alone there, wondering.

Was that . . .

"Mr. and Mrs. Bloom?" I ask out loud.

I peer down the stairs. For an instant the darkness I see there frightens me, and the knot of tension I feel inside my gut tightens further.

And then I race down into it.

☙

The creaking of the old wood under my feet as I quickly descend the stairs is the only sound, but I know that those shadows must be hiding down here.

When I reach the bottom I rush over towards the centre of the cellar—and realise a moment too late that I've put my foot on the wrong flagstone. It wobbles under my weight, and I lose my balance and fall to the ground, my knees and palms banging down hard onto the stone floor.

I feel something under my right hand, but it's so incredibly dark down here that I can't tell what it is.

I get myself up into a sitting position in the corner of the room and take a good hold of the cold, insubstantial object which keeps almost slipping out of my grasp, realising when I lift it up and run my fingers over it that it's a delicate metal chain running down to a pendant. I feel its shape and try to figure out what it might be, but can't work it out.

I lift it up and try to force myself to see whatever it is that I'm holding in the darkness, and sure enough, after a few moments my eyes finally get used to the dim light in the cellar enough for me to just about make it out.

It's a flat, rounded disk with several stems extending radially from its edges, and bearing a violet gem. It slightly resembles a sun, and it's extremely familiar to me, but I've no idea why.

I lift my eyes from the necklace—and suddenly see the two shadows.

They're standing there quietly, right in front of me. Almost invisible, but made of a different kind of darkness to the gloom in the cellar.

I scrutinise them for a moment, and when I'm almost certain that I'm sure who they are, I say again, "Mr. and Mrs. Bloom—"

But before I can get out another word, both shadows suddenly lurch forward towards me.

I recoil in fear, twisting away from them as I try to escape, but then I feel their hands on my back, colder than ice, a nightmarish touch which instantly makes me feel nauseous and vulnerable.

I start screaming, begging them to stop, but after just a few seconds all my strength abandons me, and I faint clear away and collapse down onto the cold stone floor.

DAY 24

DAY 25

DAY 26

DAY 27

WHEN I come back to my senses, the first thing I feel is the throbbing inside my head—which is also spinning vertiginously—and how sore and tired my body is.

The light from the morning sun filtering through the little window illuminates the floor around me.

What happened?

Blearily aware that I'm grasping something in one hand, I open my eyes, and when I look down at my hand I see with surprise that the necklace is still there, safe and sound. I squint at it more closely, able now to study all its details. The rays extending from the base are pointed, but one of them is missing, and a little grey patch of solder makes me think it might have been broken off. In the centre of the gemstone is carved a small A.

Without even thinking about it too much, it feels perfectly natural for me to pull the chain over my head and around my neck. I sit there staring at it for a while, although my thoughts are actually focused on what happened here.

I see again those two shadows looking at me, too blurred to be able to tell if they truly were the owners of the house—but at the same time, I can't imagine who else it could be.

I remember the pain and the fear I felt—and which still feel real, so real that I wrap my arms around myself as though trying to protect myself from something that might even not be there at all.

Maybe I'm just losing my mind.

Maybe it really is time for me to leave after all.

Overwhelmed by everything, I know that there's only one person who might be able to understand what I'm going through.

Avery.

The moment I start to stand, a sharp pain shoots up my leg from my knee, but I somehow manage to get myself to the top of the stairs, and with a huge sigh of relief I push the door shut behind me.

The entrance to the bathroom looms up in front of me, and I limp straight in to clean myself up. There's a scab forming over the graze on my knee, but there doesn't seem to be any blood anywhere else. In the mirror I notice some small purple bruises behind my shoulders where the shadows put their hands on me, but the pain that touching them causes is too much for me to deal with right now, so I put my

T-shirt back on and just wash my face with some lukewarm water.

In desperate need of some food to quiet my growling stomach, I walk down the hall to the kitchen, where everything appears completely normal.

It hardly seems possible that I've spent the night lying unconscious on a cellar floor after being attacked by phantoms.

You know what, Amethyst?

Maybe it *isn't* possible.

I grab everything edible I can find, take it all over to the couch with me, and try to get myself calmed down enough to be able to start eating.

As I pick at my food, it dawns on me how lonely I'm feeling. In the hope of finding some substitute for human company, I pick up the remote control and turn on the TV. There's a news programme on, so I start flicking through the channels in search of some cartoons or anything that might make me smile.

As I'm channel-hopping, I come across a morning TV show presented by a loud blond woman, and my finger stops dead on the button.

It's not her who's captured my attention, though.

It's the date showing at the top right-hand corner of the screen.

The twenty-seventh of October.

I look down at my feet, then back up again. How is that possible?

Where did the last three days of my life go?

Disconcerted, I search back through my memory as carefully as I can, seeking an answer to the question, but I'm positive that the last memory I have is from the twenty-third.

I've been counting the days that I've spent in this place. I'm absolutely certain.

Feeling extremely uneasy, I tiptoe over to the light switch by the front door and switch the lights quickly on and off a few times, until I see Avery's window light up as well, standing out brightly against the grey clouds dominating the sky.

⁒

"Is everything okay?" asks Avery from the other side of the gate.

At the sound of those words, it suddenly seems as though my world is falling apart, and the thought makes my eyes blurry with tears. Avery notices, but maintains his composure.

"What happened, Amethyst?" he asks, a sweet yet concerned tone in his voice.

"I . . . I don't know, Avery," I admit. A tear runs down my cheek.

"It's all right. Everything is going to be fine."

I know he's only trying to reassure me, but his words sound so fake that I cut him off. "How can you say that?"

Avery, however, doesn't seem to be listening—his eyes are staring at something which certainly isn't my face. But just as I'm really starting to get annoyed, I realize that he's staring at the necklace around my neck.

"You found it," Avery whispers, a delicate smile forming on his face.

"This?" I ask, bringing the pendant up so we can both see it.

Without saying a word, he puts his hand down the collar of his T-shirt and pulls out another that's almost identical, the only difference being that his is silver instead of gold.

"Is this Akiko's?" I wonder aloud, without taking my eyes from it.

Giving me a strange look from under his eyebrows that seems to say *Isn't it obvious?*, he nods and slips his necklace back under the white T-shirt.

I take his gesture to mean that he doesn't want to go into details, so I drop the subject, reminding myself that there are more important things we need to discuss.

Avery is gazing off into the distance, far away, at the never-ending fields of this forgotten village. His grey eyes seem darker than usual and his hair messy and tangled, but he still manages to look as imperturbable as ever.

He turns to me and I blush when he notices that I've been staring at him. To avoid making things any more awkward, I start talking.

"Where did you go the other night?"

"Can you be a bit more specific?" he asks.

"When we met," I clarify. "Down there."

"I had to go."

The fact that having abandoned me underground in that creepy tunnel on my own at night doesn't seem to bother him at all, even after everything he'd put me through during that whole infernal day of trying to convince myself to actually go down there in the first place, seems so callous and insensitive that I can't help giving a sarcastic snort.

He hears it, and adds, "I had to. I wouldn't have gone if I didn't need to."

His words sound so heartfelt, so genuine, that they make me melt. I let it go.

"But I'm here now," he concludes, reminding me that despite being the one who called him out here, I still haven't mentioned any of the things I so desperately want to talk to him about.

It occurs to me in that moment that every time we're together my brain instantly stops functioning. I can't seem to focus on anything important—instead I just try desperately to escape from the situation that I need to be dealing with.

With that in mind, I finally get to the point.

"I need to know one thing, and I need you to be honest."

He listens in silence, and so I go on.

"Did—did Mr. and Mrs. Bloom die?"

As I say the words, a wave of incredible relief at having finally got it out washes over me—but the fact that it's a distinct possibility also starts to sink in, and I realize how awful it would be if that really was the case.

Impatiently, I wait for a response.

"I don't know. But I don't think so. Honest," he says, bringing a hand to his heart.

I smile, both at his gesture and with happiness at learning that Amabel and Marvin are probably fine.

And then, in a sudden icy deluge which seems to have been designed especially to ruin this peaceful moment, rain starts to pour down, and so I hurriedly thank Avery and run back inside the house.

DAY 28

I FEEL COLD. Freezing cold. I can't stop shivering, but at the same time I feel sweaty and feverish. I roll over onto my left side, then back onto my right. I cover myself up with my blanket, only to throw it off a few seconds later. My lips are dry, and so is my throat. I raise my hands to my sweaty forehead and feel how burning hot it is.

I go on like this for hours, until I'm finally desperate enough to climb out of bed and get some water. When I do get up, though, everything starts spinning so violently that I have use the walls to keep my balance while I wobble down the corridor on shaking legs.

Surrounded by strange voices and imaginary eyes shining in the darkness, I stumble more than once as I go—but each time I force myself to get back up and keep walking until I eventually get to the kitchen, where I fill a glass with cold water and gulp it down as quickly as I can, desperate to feel better soon.

Wiping away the water dripping from the side of my mouth with the back of my forearm, I turn around, ready to go back to bed.

But then, with an awful sinking sensation, I realise that that's not what's going to happen.

There's somebody sitting in my usual place on the couch, only the back of his head visible.

"Amethyst."

A man's deep voice.

I back away, edging closer to the corridor but keeping my eyes on the figure.

He turns slightly to face me, and when his eyes lock onto mine, I freeze.

"What do you want?" I ask fearfully.

Breathing loudly in and out, the man waits a long moment before replying, but then says, "Why are you here?"

"What do you want from me?" I repeat, perplexed and feeling as though I ought to be the one asking that question. "Do we know each other?"

"You don't know me," he answers, staring at me, "but I know you."

"What do you want?" I shout, more confused than ever.

"I want you to tell me why you are here, Amethyst," he insists.

I study his appearance as much as the dim half light allows. His olive skin and black hair seem almost to merge into the gloom, and his eyes shine in the darkness, reflecting the moonlight coming in through the big windows.

"How did you get in here?" I ask. As I back off towards the kitchen, I grope along the countertop behind me for any sharp object, but, finding nothing, I keep moving until I'm at the entrance to the hall.

"That doesn't matter, Amethyst," he says, seemingly noticing how upset I am.

"Please leave," I say, lowering my voice.

He stands up. He's tall and heavyset, and I can vaguely make out that he's wearing some kind of bizarre outfit and has a shiny white scarf covered with weird symbols around his shoulders. He's also gripping something tightly between his fingers.

The necklace.

Seemingly of its own accord, my hand goes up to my throat in search of the pendant—but the delicate chain isn't there anymore, confirming that what he's holding is indeed the one that I was wearing.

He walks slowly over to the main door.

"I will leave," he says cryptically, "but you really should do the same."

He approaches the dining table and carefully places the necklace down upon it, together with a small object I can't quite make out properly.

I follow his movements without moving an inch from the entrance to the corridor. He opens the door and leaves silently, letting the front door swing shut behind him.

As soon as I hear the latch click, I rush over and place my eye to the peephole—but he has already vanished.

As I back away from the entrance I glance at the clock,

which reads 5:38, and then direct my attention to the necklace on the table and whatever it is that's half-hidden beneath it.

I place the pendant back around my neck, revealing what it was covering. A tiny object that I study for a moment in my palm: an old key. What does this open? Why would he leave it for me?

I stuff it safely into one of my pockets. I'm already standing by the light switch, so I reach over and do what Avery told me to when I needed him, expecting to see his light come on soon after as usual.

But this time, it doesn't.

๑๛

Worriedly, I slip on my shoes and get ready to make my way outside. Even though I'm still feeling shaky and light-headed, I don't take anything with me—I just want to get out of the house as quickly as possible.

The setting sun is still just visible behind the hill where, once upon a time, Alfred's house used to be. I stand there for a moment thinking about him and then set off, turning the corner of the house as I brace myself for what I'm about to do.

As I reach the gateway in the back garden, there's a debate raging in my mind: should I wait here in the hope that he turns up, or should I trespass on his property? Is this really so important that it can't wait until later—or can I just cope with it by myself?

Before I know it, though, my hand is on the wooden gate, ready to push it open.

As I expected, the gate is locked, but it's so tiny I can easily jump over it.

Or, I *should* be able to.

But when I try, something stops me halfway.

I lift my hand up in front of my face and move it forward in the air.

When it reaches the limit between our two properties, I can't move it any farther forward—it feels as though I'm pushing against some kind of incredibly powerful wind, or a barrier of soft, ghostly feathers.

An invisible wall is keeping me out.

Amazed by this force, I spend a moment staring at it—or, rather, staring at nothing—before I realize that there's something very wrong.

I'm not going to be able to get over to Avery's side of the gate, I think. And then I remember that I *was* able to meet him under the ground in the old tunnel.

Growing more and more concerned about Avery by the second, I run back inside, pull open the trapdoor by the wardrobe, and—my fears of entering that sinister place once again forgotten—race down the stairs below.

It's so dark that I can barely walk properly, and I immediately curse myself for not bringing anything with me to light my way down here, but I leave all my fears and concerns behind. It's just a long tunnel, and there's no chance of my getting lost, so, feeling my way along the walls, I simply focus on getting to where I need to be.

As I go, my eyes gradually adjust enough to make out just the barest outlines in the darkness.

I finally reach the central chamber where the three passageways meet before stretching out towards their different points of origin and stand there for a second under that iron cross, struggling to decide where to go: straight on to Avery's house, or right, towards the church?

For some reason, my instinct tells me to choose the second.

I head off along that long, gently sloping tunnel until I see a faint light growing stronger around the edges of an ancient door.

When I reach it, I shove it as hard as I can. It doesn't budge at first, but at the third try opens unwillingly, allowing me to see what's hidden behind it: the Gothic chapel whose spire I saw behind the trees my first day here, rising high and narrow from the ground and surrounded by dozens of head-stones scattered chaotically all over the graveyard, leaving just one clear path which leads right up to the entrance of the church.

I walk along the old flagstones to the church door, which bears a large sign reading, "A Safe Place for All" in Gothic lettering.

The church is built upon a hill, higher than the land where the Bloom house is located, and as I look around I realise how breathtaking the view is from here.

Hoping to get inside, I step onto the church's little porch, but the door is chained shut, and as the light of the sun is starting to fade, I take it as a sign to leave.

I walk back down the hill towards the old wooden door which gives access to the tunnel. Almost hidden by the long grass, it looks like the entrance to an abandoned storm shelter. As I pass them, I gaze absently at the gravestones lining the path, all crumbling and half-buried in weeds and ivy, except for one which I notice is newer-looking than the others.

I walk closer, almost thrust towards it, as though some kind of force were drawing me there.

And when I'm standing in front of it, something inside my mind finally snaps.

In loving memory of Avery Bradford
24/02/1990—21/10/2010
Rest in Peace

I sink to my knees.

Am I cursed?

Is that what this is? A curse?

Is *everyone* I meet dead?

I stare at the words a little while longer, then raise my head to look up at the darkening sky. My eyes are streaming with tears, and my heart feels as though it's been broken into millions of tiny, throbbing fragments.

❧

After crouching there by the gravestone for who knows how long, crying so hard that my eyes feel as though they're actually going to fall out of my head, I finally start to come back to my senses. It dawns on me how late it has got—the stars are out, and the little graveyard is lit only by the small lamp by the side of the church door.

I gather my energies, get to my feet, and pull the tunnel door shut behind me before walking back, alone, along the same tunnel I took to come here, trying to get a grip on myself as I go.

After what seems an eternity of walking, I reach the chamber halfway along the tunnel and find somebody standing there, his head lowered.

It takes me an instant to realise that it's Avery.

Still unwilling to accept his death, I run into his arms without saying a word, and he holds me, hugging me tenderly.

I've cried so much that I've got no tears left, only an avalanche of things to ask, so after relishing an embrace that I wish never had to end, and with Avery's arms still around me, I whisper my first question.

"How?"

He knows exactly what I'm referring to, and answers without hesitation. "I told you."

I lean back from him so I can look him in the face, my eyes wide open. "The fight?"

Avoiding my eyes, Avery nods.

"Why are you still here, after all this time?" I ask.

He doesn't answer, so I press him. "Is it because of your mother? You don't want to leave her on her own?"

He still doesn't make eye contact or say a single word.

"She's safe," I say. "You shouldn't have to be here. Why are you doing this to yourself?"

"Stop," he says at last.

I stand there, looking at him in shock, desperately wanting to hear his reasons.

"I can't leave. Not yet," he explains.

"But why not? Tell me, please!" I beg.

But he refuses to talk.

My shock at finding out that he is dead still fresh in my mind, and now maddened by his evasiveness and unwillingness to open up to me—even after all we've been through, even with everything that's going on—I'm suddenly overcome by a desperate, overwhelming need to get away from all this, to escape this nightmare situation.

And so I run into the dark tunnel.

Away from him.

Without looking back.

DAY 29

I CLIMB OUT of the trapdoor and throw myself down, breathless and panicky, in the corner of my bedroom, my knees pulled up to my chin, my arms hugging my legs to my body as tightly as they can, and my head hanging down.

When I open my eyes, I realise that I must have fainted from stress and exhaustion. It's 2:50 in the afternoon—a new day has begun, and I've already wasted most of it.

I stand up and in my mind run over all the things that I've learnt, wondering if maybe Avery isn't stuck in the mortal world because of his mother after all, but because of somebody else who was dear to him.

One person instantly comes to mind—his close friend Akiko.

But if that's the case, it wouldn't make any sense—it was him who told me that Akiko had died, so why would he be here if she isn't alive anymore?

I think back to all the times that I've encountered—or *thought* I've encountered—that little girl and ask myself if just maybe they *weren't* dreams. Maybe they were actually something more.

Eager to understand, I head for the Blooms' bedroom.

The ladder is still where I left it, so I climb up until I'm high enough to reach the cord hanging from the ceiling and tug down on it, opening up my way to the attic.

As soon as my eyes get accustomed to the dim light, I see the wooden chest in front of me, the framed picture still perched on top of it.

I put my hand into the pocket of my jeans and pull out the key I'd placed there for safekeeping. Sure enough, when I insert it into the lock and twist it, there's a clicking sound.

Yes.

I clear everything off the top of the chest and open the lid, nonplussed for a moment by the jumbled mass of contents that is suddenly revealed. Thrown higgledy-piggledy inside are dozens of pictures showing the young Akiko with various family members through the years. I stick my hand in and pull one out at random. On the left, there's Akiko wearing a pretty collared dress, her hair up in pigtails, while on the right a taller boy is holding her hand and smiling.

I turn the picture over and read *Akiko & Avery, 2000.*

I go through as many of the photos as I can, until I see one that I didn't expect to find: a picture of a teenage girl.

It's a close-up of her face—she isn't looking at the camera but the subtle smile on her face makes it obvious she's aware somebody's pointing it in her direction.

I know the person in this picture.

I ought to.

It's me.

I drop the picture to the floor and my heart begins beating so fast that it feels as though the already stuffy air in that cramped little space is turning solid.

My confusion at the whole bizarre situation at this point is so total, so absolute, that I completely lose it and start rummaging manically through the contents of the chest for other pictures of me.

Why would Marvin and Amabel have pictures of *me* in their house? Especially locked safely inside this box? And why would they act as though they didn't know me when we first met if they've been taking *pictures* of me all this time?

My mind is busily cranking out worst-case scenarios when I suddenly come across a picture that makes it go completely, totally blank.

It's the three of us.

I'm in the middle, standing between Mr. and Mrs. Bloom. We're all smiling, and I don't look that different from now, except maybe a few years younger.

I don't remember them taking this picture. I don't remember these people.

I just . . .

Don't remember.

The cramped attic is starting to make me feel extremely claustrophobic, so I grab a stack of pictures and, without bothering to clean up the mess I've made, get myself out of there and down the ladder as fast as I can, and race into the living room.

Once I'm sitting on the couch, I spread the pictures out across the coffee table in front of me and start giving them a quick once-over. I recognise Avery's face in a few, so I slide the others out of the way and hold one of them up in front of me.

The composition is similar to the one I saw of him when I was upstairs, but this time he looks grown up, and the girl standing next to him is not Akiko, but me.

I'm sitting there staring at it, dozens of thoughts flashing through my mind, when I realise that there's something outside the picture distracting me. I lift my eyes from the photo to the windows overlooking the back garden and see that Avery's light is on—only to go off immediately the instant I notice it.

But I'm too engrossed in the photo between my fingers to care, so I ignore what's happening outside and return to my own thoughts.

Why don't I *remember* anything about myself? Why don't I remember *any* of these people who have clearly played a role in my life?

And why do they act like they don't know *me*?

As I ask myself these questions, the thing that people have been telling me ever since I first entered this house, right since the very beginning, starts reverberating around the inside of my head.

You should leave.
The words keep echoing inside my head.
So I decide to follow their advice.

⊛

I look at the clock next to the fridge.
11:39 p.m.
I have to leave *now.*
I snatch up everything I can find—my jacket, my shoes, the necklace, the key, some of those pictures—and I'm ready to go.
I reach for the front door handle, turn it, and pull open the door, letting in a cold gust of wind.
I pause there for a moment on the doorstep and look back at the interior of the beautiful house that I've loved so much.
And then I'm ready to say my goodbyes.

DAY 30

TAKING A deep breath, I walk one final time down the pretty stone path that leads to the front gate.

I lift the latch and pull the gate open, but when I raise my foot to place it over the threshold I feel something stopping me, resisting my efforts—something like a soft, invisible wall, holding me hostage.

I keep pushing for a second, until the memory of what happened when I tried to get over into Avery's garden returns and I realise something.

I'm the one who's stuck.

In my mind, I replay my last meeting with that elderly

lady—the time when she grabbed hold of my wrist. Her warning that I would rot here forever if I didn't follow her suddenly takes on a whole new meaning.

With my heart feeling like it's about to burst inside my chest, I start kicking at the solid air, trying to break my way through the invisible obstacle that's keeping me prisoner inside the grounds of the house.

Yet despite the wild flailing of my arms and legs, I somehow manage to stay lucid enough to rationally consider what my options are. When I'm underground, I can touch Avery, and I can walk to the church. Is the tunnel a symbolic passage? Will the tunnel free me from this place?

But the hopeful excitement that starts to grow inside of me for a brief second quickly fades at the realisation that there might well be a reason for my being able to get outside and to connect to spirits belonging to other areas: the tunnel, as well as the church, currently belongs to this house and is shared with Avery's family.

That's probably why I've been able to do what I've done without coming up against the barrier—it's all part of the same property.

Exhausted and unable to come up with any other plan, I give up my attack on the invisible barrier and walk resignedly back into the house that just a few brief minutes before I'd said my farewells to.

Once inside, I turn on all the lights, sit myself down on the sofa, and dedicate myself to thinking seriously about my situation.

Hours pass.

I watch the sun rise and then eventually disappear behind the fields. And I go over everything in my mind once again:

the Blooms, the house, Avery, Akiko. Amethyst. Alfred—
Alfred.

The first ghost I'd ever met—but not the last, as it turned
out.

No one else could see him, but he looked like a perfectly
normal person to me. I could talk to him, and I could touch
him, even though he had no physical body. He could work,
and he could pick things up. He could do all of these things,
just like a real person.

The author of *Spiritual Relief*, Miss Bisset, explained that
spirits who have spent a long time in the world of the living can develop the power to interact with objects, and the
same is true of the kind of ghosts who are not aware of their
condition—the ones still clueless about their own death.

Shivering at the dark turn my thoughts have taken, I walk
over to the kitchen counter and stretch up to reach distract-
edly for a glass from the shelf.

It must be right at the back, because I can't find it anywhere.

Standing on tiptoes, I see it there, and close my hand
around it.

But my fingers pass right through it.

I can't pick it up.

I can't even feel it.

It's like it's not there at all.

My mouth hanging open in an expression of pure fear, I
back off until I'm standing in front of the shiny fridge, where
I usually check out my reflection.

But *I'm* not there.

My hands go automatically up to my mouth, and my jaw
drops even farther at the thought—

the *terrible* thought—

that I might actually be dead.

It would all make sense. All of the weird things that have been happening, my ability to talk to spirits, my dreams, my memory loss.

Everything would be explained.

But it's not the kind of explanation that I can accept.

No, I know what's happening, I really do—there's only one possible explanation. This must be a nightmare.

A nightmare!

I repeat the word to myself as I walk down the hall towards my bedroom, trying to force myself to believe it, and I'm still repeating it as I turn off the lights and curl up in my bed as though everything were perfectly normal, wrapping the blankets around me and hoping to wake up from this terrible dream.

DAY 31

A DELICIOUS AROMA of warm pumpkin pie in my nostrils wakes me up.

A new day will fix everything, I tell myself—all I need to do is just somehow to find the strength to get out of bed and face all of the things I need to deal with. I can't lie here and avoid them for the rest of my life.

I put my wrinkly clothes on and look at myself in the mirror, relieved to find that my reflection has returned and that I'm able to touch things again.

Maybe that really *was* all it was—a nightmare, nothing more.

But as I start coming out of my stupor I gradually notice that, even though *I* seem to have gone back to normal, something else has changed. The room where I find myself, the lovely shabby-chic bedroom where I've spent so much time over the last month, now looks exactly the way it did that time in my dream, with cherrywood furniture replacing the creamy shades.

Am I still dreaming? I stand in front of the wooden heart hanging on the wall, the only thing that remains unaltered, with the awful feeling that everything I'd started to believe is suddenly being thrown into doubt. Again.

I lift my finger and run it over the thick, dry paint on the bottom of the little heart: this, all of it, must be real.

I'm not dreaming, I'm sure of it.

Despite my sleepiness, I rush out of the door and down the darkened corridor that will take me to the main section of the house, and as I get closer, the powerful perfume of baking pumpkin gets stronger and stronger and voices can be heard.

"Sit down, sit down—she's coming," a woman's voice says quietly, followed by the noise of a chair scraping along the floor.

When I walk through the doorway into my favourite part of the house, I can hardly believe my eyes. Amabel is standing there in the kitchen wearing a striped apron and cooking lunch, while Marvin is sitting at the dining table with a book in his hands. Both of them have strained, forced smiles on their faces, which makes the atmosphere feel very much like it did the first—and last—time I saw them.

They seem to be waiting for my reaction, so I take a chance and ask, "Are you real?"

Marvin rises to his feet, and they both stare at me in bewilderment while I turn my gaze from the face of one to the face of the other and back again. And then, suddenly certain that they are actually, *really* there in front of me, I throw myself at Marvin, who is nearest to me. He instantly puts his arms around me, enfolding me in a protective, reassuring hug which Amabel rushes over to join.

There are so many questions in my mind, but I know that I need to make sure I get the things I've been holding inside for a month out properly.

"I'm so glad you're back—it was so nice of you to invite me in."

Amabel smiles and then gestures at the couch, saying, "I think you should probably sit down, dear."

Not unduly alarmed about whatever it is she wants to tell me, I do as she says and make myself comfortable, overcome with relief at finally seeing them again and happy to know that they're both well.

Marvin speaks first.

"Do you have any ideas about why you are here?" he asks, his face totally serious.

"Well, I . . . I just wanted to thank you both for your hospitality," I say, realizing as I say them how silly the words sound.

"Yes, dear," interjects Amabel, taking over, "but—why are you here, *now?*"

"I don't understand," I say bluntly.

Marvin takes out a picture from his pocket and slides it across the table to me.

I pick it up—it's the one I've already seen, the one where I'm standing smiling in the middle, with them on either side.

"I've already seen this," I say as I slide it back, confused as to why they want to show it to me.

"Do you know why we have it?" insists Marvin.

I think for a second, but, unable to come up with a plausible reason, I shake my head.

"Do you know who *you* are?" he continues.

"What kind of question is that?" I exclaim, beginning to feel as though I'm being interrogated.

"You should probably turn that picture over, sweetie," Amabel says with a concerned expression.

So I do, lifting my thumb from it to reveal the words *Marvin, Amabel & Akiko—2010.*

Akiko.

I look up at them, incredulous and speechless.

"Do you remember now?" Marvin asks.

"My name is Amethyst," I remind them.

"Yes, dear, I know," Amabel says, adding softly, "but that's only your *nickname.*"

"What are you talking about?" I ask.

"You never liked the name Akiko, dear—you thought that it connected you to your natural parents, and you didn't want that."

"I have no idea what you people are talking about," I snap, my jangled nerves making my voice sound rude. Confused and upset, I get to my feet, and I'm on the verge of walking out when Marvin reaches over and takes my hand.

"Please, Akiko," he says, "Hear us out—we just want to help you."

"Help me with what?" I shout. "My *name* is *Amethyst!*"

"We want you to remember," offers Amabel sweetly.

And that's when it happens.

That's when I understand that no matter how far I go, all the answers I need are in one place: here.

I sit back down on the sofa and start painfully putting the pieces together. Amabel and Marvin watch me in worried silence, until I've finished slotting all the parts into place, and it's only then that I ask them the one question I desperately need an answer to.

"Why am I here?"

"That's what we've been trying to figure out," Marvin explains. "We've been watching you, but it's hard to tell for sure."

"Your father heard a noise . . . that day. And that's when we saw you, standing out there by the gate in the rain, looking so scared," Amabel continues.

Her words bring back memories, as freshly as if they were of things that had just happened.

"And then we saw the car, one side of it all smashed up . . . and your body lying there on the ground. Lifeless," she says, as though scared to carry on.

"Wait," I interrupt her. "Are you saying that I'm dead? Because if that's what you think, I can prove you're wrong!"

I jump up and grab a book off the shelf.

"Look!" I exclaim. "I can hold things, I can talk to you two. How would that be possible if I wasn't alive?" Frantically, I look from one to the other.

"Amethyst, dear—please sit down," Marvin says gently.

I do as he asks.

"We were both . . . *surprised* to see you standing there," he starts explaining.

"Of course," I break in. "Who wouldn't be surprised to see a dead person? That's what you're trying to tell me. I get it. You think I'm dead."

"No. That's not what I meant." He breathes out loudly and then continues. "When you showed up at our door, we weren't expecting to see you."

"Why not?" I ask.

"Because you'd gone away. Almost two years before," says Amabel.

"On your eighteenth birthday, Akiko. You wanted to find your natural parents," Marvin adds softly.

I wait in silence for them to explain what it is they're telling me.

"So we decided to let you go," Marvin goes on, "a few days before your birthday. That's when we took this picture."

I try to remember a single one of the events they're describing, but my mind is completely blank.

"We couldn't do anything to help you except for giving you your parents' full names, because they never provided us with any other information. They never sent us a contact address or a phone number or *anything* after they left you with us."

"They were so young—they just couldn't take care of you properly, you see? And we could," Amabel explains.

"*Why* couldn't they?" I ask, picturing in my mind the sad faces of the couple in the framed picture on top of the wooden chest.

"They didn't explain—they were in trouble, and we were in a position to offer them some help, and so we did, without asking them anything. And it always bothered you."

"Not knowing *why* . . ." I whisper.

Marvin nods and takes up the story.

"So the day we found you standing outside the house, we knew straightaway something was wrong. And right after we saw you, we saw the car behind you, and we realised that you'd been on your way home to us right before the . . . accident. But you'd never made it."

"But if I was searching for my parents, why would I be here? Shouldn't I be halfway around the world or something?" I wonder, still not quite believing their story.

"Well, yes—that's exactly why we were so surprised to see you," Amabel explains.

I frown.

"And why should I trust you? I don't even know you," I say, still sounding a bit ruder than I actually mean to.

Marvin seems to be prepared for this question, and as soon as I finish my sentence he slides something else across the table. A newspaper.

I snatch it up and recognise the picture from the front cover of the edition which fell to the floor that day. It's the article about the accident—I knew that it had happened around here, I just hadn't bothered reading it to find out exactly where. Or to whom.

While I scan through the words, flashes of memories begin to emerge, dim at first but rapidly becoming more vivid. I remember playing in the backyard with Avery, and meeting Alfred, the new gardener, for the first time. And I remember running to Amabel in fear—fear of *him*—after hearing about the legend of the Derfla from somebody in school. I was certain that he was planning to eat me at night. So certain that at one point I started sleeping in my wardrobe.

I remember the day Avery gave me the sun necklace with the amethyst, the stone we both wear around our necks, and the promise he made to always come back to me.

I remember the day I told Amabel and Marvin that I

wanted to leave to look for my natural parents—that not knowing their reasons for giving me up for adoption was killing me inside, and that the only way for me to ever be happy would be to meet them in person.

I remember everything.

Even the day I came back here.

I was so excited to be finally getting back home. The weather was cold, but the sky was clear and the autumn air was crisp. I'd climbed aboard a train someplace far away and spent the long journey scribbling away on a notepad, trying to work out exactly what I was going to say when I finally got here. But none of the things I wrote down really managed to express what it was I wanted to tell them.

After getting off the train at the station, I'd walked all the way back to the house, watching the huddle of quaint old buildings in the centre gradually give way to the countryside as the houses grew fewer and farther between.

I'd taken my time, savouring that stroll down the cracked old pavement by the fields, until, finally, there I was—standing on the opposite side of the road, looking at the house.

I'd taken a deep breath, and started to cross.

And then the car arrived.

It was way off in the distance when I noticed it—and then suddenly it was right there, not in the distance anymore.

Out of nowhere, a silver blur, travelling so fast that it didn't seem real—so fast that I didn't even *try* to move.

Out of control.

I didn't hear the roar of its engine, only the screech of the brakes, and when it hit me the impact was so violent that it felt as though I'd been turned into white light and launched into a black hole.

And then everything was totally, absolutely black until I found myself standing in front of the Blooms' house.

"I'm grateful," I say in a quiet voice. "I need to thank you for everything that you've done for me."

I look up at them.

"And I'll never forget it. Ever again."

Tears start to stream down Amabel's peachy cheeks.

I remember everything, now. I take a deep breath and continue. "After searching for them for so long, it finally struck me—I realised that it was you two who were my real parents, nobody else. And that's why I was coming back to you. To let you know that I love you."

Even Marvin's eyes start to glisten with tears, and suddenly we are all hugging one another tightly once again. We stay that way for a long time.

It's a moment of total peace, but when it ends I still have one question left.

"How can I be talking to you, though? Are you both—" I ask, my heart racing at the idea.

"No, no, dear—we're fine," Amabel assures me immediately.

"We tried to make contact with you before, but it just never worked, so we had to wait."

"Wait for what?"

"Well, we hoped you would pick up on the hints we kept leaving you. But instead it appears that we kept scaring you away. So we just trusted that if we had you here until today, the thirty-first of October, we might be able to get through the barrier between our worlds and talk to you—and it worked, luckily," Marvin explains, sounding surprised by his own words.

I let it all sink in, and finally I understand—finally *really* understand—what all the bizarre things that have been happening to me actually were.

I open my arms again for another, longer family hug, and then, wishing that I didn't have to let go, I silently say my goodbyes to my parents.

My necklace in my hand, I walk outside. There's one more thing that needs to be done. I stand there for a moment on the porch, listening to the trees rustling and rattling in the wind.

Evening is drawing in over the fields. As I gaze off into the distance, I hear screeches of laughter approaching, and a gang of children runs into view. The one in front is clutching a pumpkin to his chest and desperately trying to keep ahead of his friends—a miniature Frankenstein's monster and a small zombie who are chasing after him, their arms held straight out in front of them, their fingers clawed in monstrous menace. A tiny ghost wearing white All Stars brings up the rear.

As they pass the house, the little phantom stops and bends over, her hands on her knees. Even through her sheet, it's obvious she's panting with exhaustion.

She stays like that for a second, then lifts her ghostly head, seemingly looking over at me. I wave. Her hand moves as though maybe she's about to wave back, but a particularly piercing squeal of amusement from the others sends her racing off in pursuit.

I watch them run along the pavement until they're out of sight, and sigh.

Time to go.

But instead of heading towards the main gate and letting myself out, I turn the corner of the house.

Avery is standing there waiting for me on his side of the gateway. Exactly as I'd imagined.

He pushes the wooden gate open for me.

When I reach for him, I feel calm and serene. Nothing worries me anymore.

He holds out his hand, and I take it.

A wry smile on his face, he says, "I told you I wouldn't leave you."

"Through the wind and through the clouds, we will rise up from the ground,
Over hills, above the trees, we will ride the breeze like bumblebees.
Hand in hand, exploring the seven seas, you and I will forever be at our ease."